SOT 3

Ron Wootters

"SOT 3," by Ron Wootters. ISBN 1-58939-935-8.

Published 2006 by Virtualbookworm.com Publishing Inc., P.O. Box 9949, College Station, TX 77842, US. ©2006, Ron Wootters. All rights reserved. No part of this publication may be reproduced, stored in a retrieval system, or transmitted in any form or by any means, electronic, mechanical, recording or otherwise, without the prior written permission of Ron Wootters.

Manufactured in the United States of America.

To:

Lt. Col. Dermott McDonald USMC

Mr. Bill Dunn   Lt.Col. J.H.(Pat) Carothers USMC(ret)

Mr. Don White   Mr. Tim Dilliplane

Di Flippi   Mr. Yoshisada Yonezuka (Yone)

                     Mr. Andy Domingo

                     1ST Sergeant Joe Keener USMC(ret)

Men I have had the privilege to serve with, be instructed by, worked for or just know.

Edited by:

Lisa D'Angelo
Book Ink Editing
www.bookink.com

In Memory of

John P. O'Neill
FBI's Chief of International Terrorism Operations
A man way ahead of the curve on the terrorist threat

CONTINUED SPECIAL THANKS TO THE MEDICAL COMMUNITY:

Dr. Richard Rathgeber D.O. Emergency Medicine
Dr. June E. Grutzmacher M.D. Ophthalmology
Dr. Douglas Boylan M.D. Orthopedic Surgery

To All Good Nurses Everywhere.

Lambertville – New Hope Ambulance and Rescue Squad
'When the siren calls the Squad is already on the way'

Doctors, PA's, Nurses and Staff at:
Buckingham Family Medicine
Joseph J. Curci, M.D., F.A.C.S
Central Bucks Cardiology
Bucks County Cardiothoracic Surgery
New Hope-Solebury Dermatology
Central Bucks Urology
Doylestown Orthopedic Specialists
Nephrology-Hypertension Specialist
Central Bucks Specialists Limited
Bucks County Medical Association / Pulmonary
Daniel J. Coletta, MD
Mark Bydalek, DMD
The Heart Center of Doylestown Hospital
Doylestown Hospital

Rosemary and I are very fortunate to live in an area where we
have access to such excellent medical care.

SOT 3
Surgeons of Terror III

PROLOGUE

I t was late winter in Naples, Italy, and with no wind blowing, the afternoon sun had it feeling more like spring.

To one man, though, the weather conditions were the last thing on his mind. He moved quickly through the side streets of an area in Naples that was always declared "Off Limits" to U.S. Sixth Fleet personnel when they were in port for liberty call.

This French Intelligence Officer was already late for a meeting because he had taken extra precautions to ensure he was not under surveillance by his own people. He knew the CIA was watching. They had discovered weeks ago, he was a double agent and since money was the reason for him being a traitor, they made him a better offer to work for them. Since they explained performing a Houdini and disappearing was his alternative, he accepted.

Using him would get much needed intelligence on Middle East extremists groups, but the CIA operatives in no way trusted him. He was kept under surveillance 24/7 and when scheduled for a meeting with his Middle East friends, Agency medical people implanted listening devices in some creative places in case he neglected to relay some information.

Unknown to the triple agent, the listening device would not be turned on until after the meeting had started. This was done to

1

avoid detection in case security devices were being used to scan meeting members as they arrived. When to turn on the device was a guesstimate. CIA surveillance would notify their people when he entered the place of the meeting. The Case Officer would allow enough time for him to clear any security before ordering the device to be turned on. Since the triple agent thought the device was on all of the time, he would probably report anything that was not picked up at the beginning of the meeting.

It was a good thing this procedure was in place because some unannounced Middle East types attended with their security team scanning individuals as they arrived. In addition to the new faces, Hezbollah and drug/terrorist groups were also represented.

"Must you always be late, Pierre?" the Hezbollah representative inquired, as the French traitor entered the meeting room.

"Would you rather I not take precautions to ensure I am not under surveillance?" the Frenchman fired back.

"We may be at fault for his being tardy," a new face at the meeting volunteered. "Two of our security team followed him to the meeting until he eluded them."

The Frenchman acknowledged the man's words in agreement. *'The fact he had been unaware of the surveillance and eluded them using techniques he had developed over the years didn't bother him. What really had him wondering was when did the men start following him, before or after his visit with U.S. Intel?'*

"Very well," the Hezbollah rep stated and called the meeting to order. "We are here, along with our new friends, to revisit this problem. As you all know, someone has been eliminating our cells around the world that supply us with funds to support our struggle. They may have also been responsible for the assassinations in Iraq and that has gotten the attention of our new friends. We will first get an update from Pierre, then we will discuss the matter in detail."

With that, the Frenchman stood and began his report. "I have been in contact with members of Western Intelligence trying to get information about this new force, but have had no luck. Some people like to talk and impress others, but I can't even get a hint from them. At first, I thought the group either had very deep cover or were contractors being used by the government, but after the assassinations in Iraq, I am not convinced that was the case."

"From what I see in the media, you French people have a clandestine unit that fits the description," another new face inquired.

"To answer your question, yes, and at the same time, no." The Frenchman shook his head. "There was an incident on Corsica not long ago where two former U.S. Intelligence Officers were rescued and heavy losses were inflected on their abductors."

"I remember reading about that," the Hezbollah rep exclaimed. "The paper stated it was a French clandestine unit."

"That's what had me wondering," Pierre replied. "I looked into the matter very extensively and no French clandestine units were involved in the rescue. Someone kept giving the credit to the French government and they were so happy about all of the good public relations, they didn't care if it wasn't true."

"Do you feel we should pursue the matter?" the Hezbollah rep inquired.

"Yes," Pierre quickly replied, trying not to bring any suspicion to himself, "and the starting point should be the two retired agents. Someone rescued them for a reason and that reason may lead us to the organization. We will have to locate the men, interrogate them, and have a strike force available to destroy the group if it was the one in question."

"That sounds like something we can take care of," one of the new faces offered.

"Al-Qaida has developed teams that will strike at its enemies around the world. The first Team is ready and killing these dogs would send a message to the west that we have arrived."

CHAPTER ONE

J and Mac didn't have much to say during dinner at a local restaurant. Due to their current venture, they couldn't talk about the job out in public as most people did, but the silence continued during the drive back to the residence.

Finally, Mac broke the silence with, "Looking back, I still can't believe we pulled off that last Project."

"Figured that was the reason you were so quiet this evening," JJ replied. "To tell you the truth, the last two Projects have been on my mind."

"Have you given much thought about the long term?" Mac inquired.

"What do you mean?" JJ asked.

"The Team, the Board, the Projects," Mac answered.

"Why, is it starting to wear you out?" JJ asked, concerned.

"Wasn't really thinking about myself or the Board," Mac replied. "It's the Team. How long can they do what they do before burnout?"

"Why, are you seeing signs of burnout?" JJ asked again with even more concern.

"No, no," Mac answered, "but you have to wonder."

"I think we will be okay. They are all topnotch professionals," JJ assured Mac.

"You are probably right," Mac conceded. "They are a very special group."

"I agree, and am sure at this very moment each man is off somewhere unwinding by either raising hell or is at some restful place relaxing and enjoying themselves.

***

Two pair of eyes in the darkness watched Tic's every move, as he relaxed on a bench just inside a small city park.

During Tic's one month leave, he was on a voluntary mission to help wipe out disease that was running rampant over the land. Not being that familiar with this country, he did not rush into something that would be ineffective or maybe make things worse, so he took time to prepare and get to know the area in this dangerous land. Tic had done his homework and was ready to initiate his plan to help wipe out this dreaded disease.

This night of the week, the leader of this Colombian death squad always went to visit his *puta*. For that reason, he had only one bodyguard with him and Tic would take advantage of that fact.

Tic looked very casual as he waited. He smoked a cigarette, had a bottle in a paper bag that he pretended to sip on from time to time, and faked a nap as he sat on a bench across the street from the whore's apartment. Tic felt he blended right into the neighborhood, but it was getting late and he began to wonder if his prey had gotten delayed on business or for some other reason.

Tic's thoughts were interrupted by the sound of a vehicle coming down the side street next to the apartment building.

As it turned the corner, he recognized it to be the death squad leader's car and Tic was on the move.

It was obvious to the eyes in the darkness the man was moving due to the arrival of the car and they were on the move as well.

When the body guard brought the car to a complete stop, Tic was standing by the passenger window with gun in hand and shot the driver twice with a silenced 9 millimeter, killing him instantly. As Tic turned toward the back seat, his primary target had already gotten out and was running across the street in the direction of the small park.

Tic ran around the back of the car and gave chase to the fleeing man when a jeep carrying four members of the death squad appeared from around the corner. Tic looked, but didn't stop to consider the situation knowing if he surrendered, he was a dead man.

The death squad leader also looked, realized the man chasing him was between him and the four men in the jeep, and yelled for the men to help him.

Tic ran to the other side of the street and was about to enter the small park when two men from the darkness appeared out of nowhere. Tic quickly turned to his right and engaged them when a voice said, "Easy, Zorro."

Tic had a look of disbelief on his face for a moment, then continued his pursuit.

The four men from the jeep were in the middle of the street when Blue Jay and Bean took aim and downed the two in front, then quickly dispatched the other two.

After they were sure no movement was coming from the four men in the street, Bean and Blue Jay proceeded into the park to locate their teammate. About twenty yards into the park, they heard footsteps rapidly approaching their location. Not knowing for sure who it was, both men knelt down and pointed their weapons in the direction of the noise. They didn't have to wait long before Tic appeared. He was running back to make sure they were not having problems with the four men.

"Did he get away?" Bean inquired.

"No," Tic answered, "he won't be killing anymore innocent people."

"Good, let's mogate," Blue Jay suggested.

With that, the three men moved off to their right through the small park to a city street. After walking several blocks and making sure no one was following, they picked their not so new transportation. Blue Jay hotwired a car parked on the street and they were on their way.

As the car found its way through the city heading toward the waterfront, Tic broke the silence with a question. "So you two came all the way down here to watch my back?" he inquired.

"Yep," Bean answered.

"Well that, plus we want you to make something go boom," Blue Jay added with a smile.

"Don't listen to this turkey," Bean reassured Tic. "We noticed back at the Barn something was on your mind. At first, we thought it was that last Project. When it continued after it was completed, we knew it was something else and that it was serious.

"Blue Jay noticed you looking at a picture of a priest a few times. We put two and two together and decided to follow you. When we found out your destination, we just figured out the rest."

"Who was the priest?" Blue Jay inquired.

"My uncle," Tic replied. "He was a good man with no political preference; he just wanted to help the people."

"I'm afraid that's becoming the norm down here," Bean offered. "Some people have no regard for priests or any type of religious people."

"Not to change the subject," Tic interrupted, "but how are you two getting out of the country? My escape route is only for one, so one of you can use it."

"We think that escape route is bogus," Blue Jay replied. "That man you were dealing with was reporting back to what looked like a headquarters of some type."

"Are you sure?" Tic inquired. "Do you think you could find that building again?"

"I think so," Blue Jay said, as he looked around to get his bearings.

After a few turns the car was driving past the building in question.

"That's the one," Bean told Tic, as he pointed to a building.

"Yes, you are right," Tic confirmed. "It's HQ for one of the death squads."

After the stolen car had driven on about another block, a big explosion was heard that shook the area buildings, but caused no damage to them. That was not true for the building in question, as the entire front of the structure came crashing down into the street.

"When I said we wanted you to make something go boom that was not what I had in mind," Blue Jay scolded.

"Maybe those bastards will think twice next time," Tic answered, as he wiped a remote triggering device free of fingerprints then threw it out the window.

***

When the car reached the waterfront, it stopped. The three men got out, walked two blocks, then down an old stone stairway that led to the edge of the water, and waited.

A short time later, the sound of a powerful racing boat engine could be heard and within seconds, it had slowly pulled up alongside the three men and allowed them to board.

"You, too," Tic inquired with a big smile.

"Yeah," Check replied. "Anything to get a chance to drive one of these boats. Ever since I stopped racing, I don't get out much. You remember, back when I used to kick your ass on a regular basis during the racing season."

"Wish he hadn't said that," Blue Jay relayed to Bean.

"I know," Bean replied. "Let's find a sturdy seat."

The boat quietly moved off and with no running lights on disappeared into the darkness. Once Check felt they were at a safe distance, he brought the boat up to a fast speed and settled in for a long trip.

A few minutes had passed at that speed when Tic inquired, "Are we planning to get anywhere soon?"

"They told me to keep it respectable," Check replied.

"Oh, it's respectable all right. At this pussy speed you couldn't call it anything else."

"I really wish Check hadn't said that about their racing days," Blue Jay again relayed to Bean.

"Pussy speed it is," Check said. As he pushed the throttles further down, the boat started skipping across the water.

After Check picked up the trio, he headed out to sea before turning north. Doing this made it harder for them to be detected. Since Check was unfamiliar with this area, he did not realize the Colombian coastline curved to the left as it headed north, and being a rural part of the country, there were no lights on shore to alert him that the coastline was getting closer. As the boat raced north, Check and Tic were reminiscing about their racing days when a patrol boat popped out of an inlet right in front of them. Having their running lights turned off the patrol didn't even see them coming, but at the speed the boat was going, it probably wouldn't have mattered much anyway.

"Hold on," Check alerted Blue Jay and Bean, as he turned the wheel to the left faster than he normally would. The boat leaned to its left as it responded to the command.

"It's going to be close," Tic observed, as the distance between the two boats quickly closed.

"We'll get passed as long as he doesn't do anything stupid," Check observed.

The patrol boat didn't see them until they were right on top of them. The helmsmen was wondering what all of the commotion was about and looked out the window to his left.

His eyes opened wide when he saw a boat speeding right for them. His first thought was to speed up to avoid a collision. Unfortunately, that was the stupid thing Check was talking about. The helmsman's brain kept ordering speed up, but his hands were frozen to the wheel and before he could get them free, it was too late. The oncoming boat was heading right for the bow of the patrol and a collision was imminent.

Tic knew if he turned the wheel any harder, they might capsize, but he had no choice. He used the wheel like a surgeon used his scalpel, very precise, not too much, but not too little. The boat again responded to the command and allowed them to squeak by the bow of the patrol with only a few inches to spare.

Needless to say, this did not make the lieutenant on the patrol boat very happy for two reasons. One, he knew his boat could not even come close to catching the other vessel. And two, he had to stop and retrieve a few of his men that had jumped overboard in anticipation of a crash.

Check did not turn back north after the near collision with the patrol boat, but kept heading out to sea.

"That coastline snuck up on me," Check confessed. "I'm taking her further out."

A short time later, the boat was again heading north and Bean inquired, "So was that the usual racing day type thing?"

"Sort of," Tic replied, "but we try to get a little closer on racing day."

Check gave Tic a big smile knowing Blue Jay and Bean would be yelling up additional comments from the back seat.

***

The lieutenant on that boat they almost sideswiped might not be able to catch them, but he had a radio and other patrol boats were in the area, some equipped with radar.

Being further out to sea and moving along at a reasonable speed, the group had settled in for a long ride, but was showing up on someone's radar screen.

"Moving at that rate of speed it must be the boat we were alerted about," the captain of a second patrol boat told his radar operator. "It is too fast for us, but we have radar and a deck gun, that should even things up," he announced. The captain then set a head-on intercept course for the speeding vessel and alerted all hands.

Check and Tic had gotten real quiet and the two back seat drivers were wondering why. "You two run out of gab?" Bean inquired.

"No," Tic replied. "We're not sure, but we may have something coming our way."

Blue Jay and Bean moved next to the other men to help with the search.

"There," Tic said, as he pointed to red and green lights directly ahead of them.

"Maybe they want to play chicken?" Check wondered out loud.

"What are our options?" Blue Jay inquired.

"The first thing we should probably do is make a course change to see if he has radar and is looking for us. Right, boat captain?" Tic asked Check.

"We could do that," Check agreed, "but I'd say he has radar and wants to play chicken."

"Well, just in case, could we make a course change?" Blue Jay asked.

"No problem," Check complied, as he turned the boat seaward.

As the boat sped seaward, the green and red lights could still be seen in the distance, but a short time later, only the red light could be seen.

"They have radar," Tic announced. "They changed course to intercept us."

"Told you they want to play chicken," Check reminded the others.

"So what should we do now?" Blue Jay asked.

"If he wants to play chicken I hate to disappoint him," was Check's reply before letting out a big laugh.

After his chuckle, Check started to explain his tactics. "By the looks of the beam on that boat he is probably big enough to carry a deck gun of some sort. We would have to stay out of range when we try to get past him and we don't have the fuel. Besides, if we ran parallel to him and he leads us just right, one of the shells from his deck gun could take us out before we saw it coming." Check then explained his plan to the other three.

"Sounds reasonable," Blue Jay agreed, as he looked at Bean.

"We'll be back here if you need us," Bean announced, as both men returned to their seats.

Once again, the boats were on a collision course, but this time it was planned by both boats. As the range between the two crafts shortened, the captain of the patrol boat fired a range finder shell from his forward deck gun and it fell short.

Check maintained his speed and waited for the next shell to be fired.

After a little adjustment, the patrol fired again. The shell came closer and Check increased the speed of the boat.

The third shell went over and landed well behind the boat.

Check then increased to full speed all of the time closing the distance between the two boats.

The next shell also went long, but not as far as the previous one.

"Time for a change in tactics," Check informed Tic, as he turned the wheel to starboard a little then back.

Now instead of going head to head they were a little to the left of the gunboat.

The gunboat fired again, but if the shell was on target, nobody was there.

Check figured the radar operator had notified the captain of their course change, so after a long pause he performed the same maneuver to port putting them on the other side of the gunboat.

The captain realized it would be too difficult to hit this boat with his deck gun so instead had his men assembled amidships while he communicated with his radar operator. The operator told the captain the same maneuvers were being performed. If it kept doing the same thing at that speed and distance, the oncoming vessel would probably pass them on the starboard side of the patrol boat.

The captain ordered all hands to take up position on the starboard side and to prepare to fire on the boat as it passed. He then ordered all search lights turned on and to track the oncoming vessel.

When the search lights came on Check yelled to the back of the boat, "Got a minute?"

In a split second, Bean and Blue Jay were standing next to Check and Tic. "We have to try and take out those lights when we get close enough," Check informed the other three.

The men took out their 9 millimeters and removed the silencers. That would give the rounds more velocity when fired.

Check again performed the maneuver and seemed to let the boat drift a little more to starboard before he straightened it out.

After the radar operator on the patrol boat informed the captain, the incoming boat had time for one more maneuver. He took up a position next to the forward deck gun and ordered it to minimum elevation. It would be like a lucky shot, but the captain figured he would fire on the vessel as it crossed his bow.

"Anytime with those lights," Check yelled and within a few seconds, all three men began to fire at the searchlights.

The larger one was knocked out quickly, but from a boat bouncing across the water, the smaller one was proving to be more difficult. The three men finally saturated the area with rounds and one of them found its mark. The searchlight made a bright flash before going dark and Check took a long pause before again turning the boat to port.

Without searchlights, the captain had to rely on his radar operator to give the boat's location. "He's started to turn to his portside, captain," the excited radar operator yelled.

"Good," the captain replied, trying to control his anticipation.

The oncoming boat was about to cross the bow of the patrol boat when Check said, "Four, five," then spun the wheel back to starboard and within seconds, they passed the patrol boat on its port, not the starboard side.

The captain tried to reposition his men, but with all of those incoming 9 millimeter rounds plinking and bouncing all over the place, the crew was a little reluctant to take up positions on the port side.

The three men were not trying to hit anybody, just trying to create a little distraction until they got past the patrol boat. They seemed to be successful.

"Tell me which way he turns," Check yelled to the others.

The captain of the patrol boat ordered a hard turn to starboard so he could get a few shots with his deck gun.

When the running lights changed from red and green to green only, Tic yelled, "He's turned to starboard."

Check reacted immediately and turned his wheel to starboard. Since he turned in the same direction, more time would pass before the patrol boat could get his deck gun into firing position and time meant distance to the speed boat.

"Talk to me," Check yelled to the others.

"He's still coming around," Tic replied.

A few seconds later, Tic yelled, "Green and red," and Check turned the wheel to port.

The patrol boat had already fired a shell, but it wasn't even close. It was obvious they were in the clear so they resumed their original course.

"Well that was interesting," Blue Jay commented.

"I agree," Bean concurred. "The sort of thing that will put a racing stripe into the shots of the fainthearted."

"It wasn't even close," Check replied.

"What do we have onboard, a couple of landlubbers?" Tic inquired.

"We have to enroll in that mail order Explosives School we saw advertised on that matchbook cover," Blue Jay suggested to Bean. "Then the next time Zorro goes out for vengeance we won't have to go save him."

Needless to say, the remainder of the trip was not a quiet sea voyage.

CHAPTER TWO

The Board was in session for the first time since the completion of their largest Project to date and since that Project stretched the Team and Board to their limits, a review of resources and manpower were in order.

JJ had just completed his presentation of financial and other Board resources with all in agreement with his findings.

General Mac was next to present an evaluation of the Team he and JC, the Team leader, had developed.

"As JJ said, we are all aware of the strain in both finances and physical resources the last Project put on the Board and Team," Mac announced, as he started his presentation. "It was something that needed to be done, but a lot bigger than any of us had in mind when we started taking on these Projects. With that said, I will give you our findings. JC and I evaluated each area and member of the Team. You are already aware of some of what I am about to say, but please bear with me and feel free to air any questions or concerns."

"Team total, eleven. Team Leader, JC, retired Marine Corps Colonel, pilot, expert with weapons, and our main gizmo man. Blue Jay, Field Team Leader if JC is not present, contract type, prior to that Marine Corps, CIA. During several tours in Japan while in the Corps attended martial arts and other schools that gave him special skills and abilities. Getting in and out of places without being seen is one that we have already used several times. Bean, part-time contractor type, prior Army Airborne Ranger, Special Forces, and CIA. Benz, Japanese, expert in martial arts, been in the contract business for many years. Panda, Philippino, also martial arts, takes on contracts from time to time. Regular occupation, engineering consultant. Check, Arab, explosives, takes on contracts from time to time, owns a Middle East restaurant. Tic, Cuban, explosives, also part-timer, regular occupation, stockbroker. Bris, French, primarily a contractor, but also an artist and a good one. Pru, English, contractor, long-range shooter. Met, German, also a contractor, long-range shooter. Air Jockey, contractor, can fly helicopters, most prop aircraft, the corporate jet, and able to function as a Team member on the ground if needed.

"In the area of primary weapons, we will continue with the Heckler & Koch MP5 with the 9 millimeter Beretta pistol as the sidearm. Long-range shooters will be using the .50 cal Barrett M82a1m semiautomatic. When we first started the Projects, we employed a bolt action version of the fifties. The bolt action is an excellent sniper weapon for a one-shot, one-kill situation, but we found out early on when the long-range shooters are in support of the Team, they were taking down targets as fast as their spotters could find them. For that reason, we are staying with the semi-automatic.

"Since the Projects are executed on foreign soil, for the most part, language plays an important part, and at least one Team member can converse in the following languages: English, Japanese, Philippino, French, Spanish, Arabic, German, and a few languages from the old soviet block countries.

"Both JC and myself felt we were pretty well covered except in the pilot area. Air Jockey is our primary, but if anything happened to him, it could put us in a bad way especially if we are out on a Project. To help correct this," Mac continued, "with Air Jockey as our instructor, JC took a refresher on flying the helicopter and I tackled the jet."

"You flew the jet?" JJ interrupted.

"Yes, I flew the jet," Mac replied quickly. "Remember those golden wings I used to wear on my uniform? I flew only prop aircraft back then, but with Air Jockey and JC's help, I can now fly the corporate jet. Besides, it's not like the FAA will know about it and require a license."

"Forgot about the wings," JJ apologized. "Withdraw the question."

Presentation completed, Mac asked for questions or concerns.

Everyone seemed to agree with the findings and were about to move onto the next item on the agenda when Gil Dunn spoke up.

"I have a question, addressed to both Team and Board, but mostly to the Board," Gil started. "When the Projects began, they were very effective, but small compared to what was going on in the world at the time. I'm sure the last two Projects, especially the last one, have caused blips on both friend and foe's radar screens. I think this question is directed mostly toward the Board since I'm sure this Team is already aware of what I am about to say.

"Do you all realize from now on it will get even more dangerous? I ask this because sometimes people get into things and go with the flow not realizing it was becoming more and more dangerous."

"I'm glad you asked that question, Gil," JJ replied. "Since I'm the one that got you all involved in what we are doing, it has been a constant concern for me. Let me echo Gil's question. Do you all realize?"

Each Board member looked at their fellow Board members and without conversation all acknowledged with a "yes."

With that, Jeff Dawson spoke up. "We all appreciate your concerns and of making us aware of the dangers, but I think each member is aware and stays aware of the dangers of what we are doing. And as for you, JJ," he continued, "we are successful, worldly, and independent people. If we didn't want to get involved in this we would have told you no when you first asked us."

The Board members all agreed with Dawson's statement and reassured JJ.

The third item on the Board's meeting agenda was presented by Mr. Wilson. He proposed the Board and Team finally meet in person. The Board knew each man on paper by code name only, but had never met them due to security regulations that were put in place when the Board and Team were formed.

For a while, it looked like the motion might have had a chance of passing until JJ, the founder of the group, again aired one of the original reasons for having separation. If one group were compromised for any reason, the other group would still maintain its anonymity.

That signaled the start of round one. The Board usually agreed on issues after discussing them, but if any one of them felt strongly about an issue, it was clear the decks for action. That was one of JJ's criteria when he handpicked the original Board members and for when he and General Mac recruited Admiral Fox after his retirement. JJ figured if everyone was saying the same thing all of the time, a group could get off course and not even realize it.

As the debate continued, two sides formed. John Howard, President of Zerk Pharmaceutical, Jeff Dawson, President of International Oil, and Charles Wilson, President of Wilson

Explosives Company on one side, and Mac, retired Marine Corps General, Foxie, retired Navy Admiral, and JJ on the other side with Gil Dunn, President of Van Corcoven Firearms Company and former DDO at CIA, undecided.

The meeting didn't get heated, but it got a little warm before JJ finally called for a vote. Four to three and that meant the only communications between Board and Team would still be through JJ or Mac.

The third item resolved, the Board moved onto number four and again Wilson requested permission to speak.

'This is so unlike Charley,' JJ thought to himself, as he granted him permission. *'Propose something that gets voted down and then follow up right away with something else you want that may have a hard time getting passed, and hope the other members will now feel obligated to vote with you. Boardroom tactics. Can hardly wait to hear this one.'*

Wilson proposed that since the Board was making recommendations for Projects that seemed to be getting bigger and bigger, the Board should have a better understanding of what is expected of the Team in the areas of tactics, firearms, etc. This would put the Board more in tune with the Team. Wilson ended by saying, "I realize the Team had the final yes or no on any Project, but they have yet to say no and I feel that puts more responsibility on the Board when submitting Projects to the Team."

JJ knew there was more to this proposal than Charley was saying, but since he had won the last battle, agreed when the Board voted in favor of the idea.

After the vote, the planning started. Gil Dunn would provide the weapons, with Foxie and Mac setting up and conducting the training sessions. When the Team was first formed, they used JJ's cabin in rural Pennsylvania for initial training and it was decided that would be a good place for the Board to train.

"Okay, are there any other items?" JJ asked the Board members.

"What type of weapons?" Charles Wilson asked.

"What?" JJ asked.

"What type of weapons will we be using?" Wilson rephrased his question.

"Probably MP5's," Gil Dunn fielded the question. "Why, do you have a preference?"

"I always liked the Sub Thompson," Wilson replied.

"You mean the Thompson Submachine gun, right?" Gil inquired.

"Yes, that's the one. I always called it the Sub Thompson," Wilson confirmed.

"I'm sure I could find one, but wouldn't you prefer a more modern weapon like the MP5?"

"They are good, but I would prefer the .45 caliber. More knockdown power," Charles replied.

"More knockdown power." Gil echoed Wilson's words. "I suppose you would prefer the five hundred round drum magazine as well?"

"Two if you don't mind," Wilson replied. "They tend to jam."

"Two if you don't mind," Gil again echoed Wilson's words, as he made a reminder note for himself. "Wilson, you realize these weapons are just for training purposes at JJ's cabin?"

"I know," Charles Wilson confirmed.

"And it was such a pretty wooded area," JJ reflected.

"Until Wilson the forest slayer showed up," Dawson instigated.

"After the forest he'll probably turn the Thompson on the weeds," Mac added. "Maybe that should be his code name, Weed Whacker."

"Oh yeah," Charles responded. "Then you can be the Tally Whacker."

With order finally restored and the initial plan completed, JJ looked at Wilson and inquired, "Is this pain in the ass thing making its way around the table? First it was Mac, now you."

"No, no," Charles replied with a big grin on his face. "Just trying to get more in touch with the troops."

"Me?" Mac asked with fake surprise. "I didn't do anything. Unless you're still mad about that Charley Tuna and the weapons thing?"

"Don't even bring that up!" JJ commanded, as the Board members all smiled.

"I hope it doesn't get around to you, Dawson," JJ said. "You and Howard are two of the few that haven't given me grief."

"Well, there was that issue about meeting the Team," Dawson replied.

"But that got voted down," Howard quickly added. "Maybe we should request to become pen pals with the Team."

JJ looked at both men then at Foxie and said, "It's a mutiny."

"Looks that way," Foxie replied. "Is that chocolate cake I see back by the coffee pot?"

"Yes, it's chocolate cake," JJ confirmed. "Go have some and take these hemorrhoids with you."

Everyone including JJ laughed, as they all moved to the chocolate cake and coffee area.

CHAPTER THREE

O ne week had passed since the Team returned to home base, AKA, The Barn. JJ and Mac had called a meeting to present a new Project to the Team and all were seated in the training room. As in the past, JJ would present the Project then Mac would cover the operational side.

"Good morning, men," JJ started.

"Morning," was the group's reply.

"First, I want to again commend you all for an excellent job during our last colossal undertaking. For a small group like this to accomplish such a large Project was truly remarkable." The Team acknowledged the kind words and JJ continued the briefing.

"As in the past, we will field all questions at the end of both presentations."

"Hopefully this Project will not be as demanding or dangerous. The Board selected it due to its importance to the terrorist network, but as in the past, you have the right to decline for any reason. With that said, I'll give you the overview." JJ continued. "As you all know, Hezbollah has been implicated in the counterfeiting of U.S. dollars and European currencies, both to finance its operations and to disrupt Western economies by impairing international trade and tourism. We are mostly concerned about the, 'to finance its operations' part. If we disrupt some of their financial operations, it could mean less weapons and explosives for their people or a least a delay. According to the U.S. Treasury Department, Assad Ahmad Barakat has close ties with Hezbollah leadership and has worked closely with numerous Islamic extremists and suspected Hezbollah associates in South America's tri-border area (TBA) made up of Brazil, Paraguay, and Argentina.

"The Treasury Department's press release in two thousand four caused their counterfeiting operations to be relocated. Through the Board's resources, we have discovered the operations were moved to just inside the U.S. border with Mexico. At that time, it was a good move, but lately with all of the immigration problems things were getting too busy in their area so they are probably going to move everything. If we are going to hit it, we have to consider two things. One, we will have to move fast and two it is on U.S. soil.

"I realize that was very brief, but that's about it in a nutshell." JJ continued. "Mac will present the high level operations side of the Project."

Mac moved to the front of the room and started his portion of the presentation. "I want to echo JJ's words about the last Project, but with a group like this I'm not that surprised."

These were nice gestures coming from JJ and Mac especially since they were also in the field with the Team during the last Project and made important contributions to the operational side.

"As JJ said this one was on U.S. soil." Mac continued. "We again have to watch out for both friend and foe for obvious reasons. We feel the key is to keep it as low profile and quiet as possible. Take out the operation without blowing up the entire facility and without a firefight erupting. All of our weapons will be silenced, but we can't be sure about the security force around the counterfeiting facility. Have learned from past experience not to go into great detail because you just take it and rework the shit out of it, so I have decided to just give you an operational overview and let you all work out the details or as JJ said, Just point them in a direction and turn them loose."

Everyone including JJ chuckled at Mac's humorous, but true, remark.

"I guess we are ready for questions," Mac announced and JJ joined him at the front of the room.

"Let's get some clarification on this." JC started the question phase. "We can destroy the operation without blowing it up, but what about the people?"

"They must be taken out," JJ responded. "The security force for obvious reasons, but you must get the brains behind the counterfeiting so they cannot set up shop elsewhere."

"What about the bodies?" Blue Jay inquired.

"Since it will be inside the U.S. speed is very important. I suggest maybe a drug deal gone bad scene?"

The question and answer phase went on for a few minutes more when Met asked, "Can you tell us the exact location of this facility?"

"We purposely held that back due to it being on U.S. soil," JJ answered. "We would first like to get a tentative answer from the Team. If the answer is yes, we will give you the exact location. If no, there was no need to know. We realize you will require time to discuss this so we can meet again later if you like."

"Just a minute," JC interrupted, as he quickly canvassed each member of the Team. A few seconds later JC again spoke. "I think we can give you a tentative yes on this one? Am I right, men?" JC asked the Team.

The group replied in favor of JC's question, so JJ continued with the exact location. "Nogales, Arizona," JJ said. "East

International Street, Nogales, Arizona to be exact." He continued. "You will be in urban surroundings for this one."

"I say, it may be better than being out in a rural area with all of the border patrol watchers and their night vision gear," Pru added while everyone agreed.

After a few more questions, the meeting was adjourned. Everyone filed out of the room and headed for the main house for lunch.

JJ, Mac, and the Team entered the house through the back door and proceeded through the kitchen on their way to the dining room and the oversized table JJ had special made so the Team, House Team, Mac, and himself could all take their meals at the same time.

Top Kiner, Lady1 and LadyA were putting the finishing touches on lunch and greeted them as they all entered the kitchen.

Air Jockey wanted to keep up the traditional salutations after the entire Team returned from furlough and said, "So, Top still watching Emeril and if so will things improve?"

Top Kiner was busy tending to what was in the oven and mumbled something in reply.

"How's that!" Jockey inquired, trying to be a smart ass.

"I'm a little busy; don't want to overcook your lunch," Top replied.

"Like we could tell if that happened," Jockey fired another volley.

"You could tell," Top Kiner replied, as he remained very intent on what was going on in the oven and requested someone to hand him a very large spoon that was hanging from a rack along with other utensils.

Air Jockey was eager to assist, and removed the giant spoon from the rack and handed it to him.

Top took the spoon by the handle and immediately crowned Jockey on the top of his head with it. The metal sound of the spoon vibrating could still be heard as Top said, "Behave."

An instant uproar occurred in the kitchen as everyone burst into laughter. They all knew something humorous was going to happen, but Top surprised them all with his change in tactics.

Jockey, still rubbing his head, finally said, "I never liked Marines."

"Good," Top replied with a smile on his face, as he continued to watch what was going on in the oven.

When the laughter subsided everyone moved into the dining room to enjoy his or her usual good meal.

During the meal, Pru broke the silence with a question. "I just realized something. I know we all have code names for obvious reasons, but I always wondered why the ladies code names were Lady 1 and Lady A."

"I really wish he hadn't asked that question," Blue Jay relayed to Bean who was sitting next to him.

Bean just smiled as JJ and Mac started to tell about their first meeting with the ladies, the controversy about code names, and the reason they finally settled on Lady 1 and Lady A.

By the time JJ and Mac finished telling the story, with the ladies making comments and group laughter breaking out along the way, it was time for dessert, Double Dutch Chocolate Cake. This was Air Jockey's favorite and Top made sure he got a giant piece.

As he looked at the huge piece he was served Jockey said, "I always did like Marines."

***

SOT 3

Ten days had passed since JJ and Mac presented the new Project. A business jet had just landed at a small airport not far from Nogales, Arizona.

Two of the Team members, Pru and Met, had arrived in Nogales two days earlier to check out the situation. Per Team SOP, the two men did not travel together. They had separate airlines, separate rental cars, and separate rooms, but at the same hotel.

As Pru maintained surveillance at East International Street, Met drove to the small airport to brief the Team.

Since the Project was in an urban area on U.S. soil, JC would act as field team leader at a command post close by.

Doing that would allow Blue Jay to focus more on taking out the facility while JC monitored the area and supplied information about friend and foe coming and going.

After Met briefed the Team on the plane, they unpacked their weapons. This time out, Met and Pru would be in support using the Remington 308. It wasn't like the .50 caliber they have used on previous Projects, but it would get the job done.

Following the plan, Air Jockey stayed with the plane while the rest of the Team loaded up in two SUV's that were waiting at the airfield. The Board had many bogus accounts set up for such things and the bills were always paid, but if a trace was done, it always led to a dead-end.

JC traveled with Met, picked up Pru, and set up an observation post at a selected location. Benz and Panda usually acted as spotters for Pru and Met, but this time joined the others and JC served as spotter for both shooters. It was about nine P.M. when JC, Met, and Pru took up positions on a hill overlooking a stand alone building on East International Street. >From their vantage point, the three men could cover the back and both sides of the building. The Team would enter through the back and in the unlikely event someone got away, that person would have to go to their left or right, putting them into Pru or Met's rifle scope. They could run straight, but since the border with Mexico was about a street width from the front of the building, they wouldn't get far.

The Intel the Board supplied stated that during the day, the building was a legitimate print shop and the daytime employees were unaware of the counterfeiting operation or the fact they were working for people with terrorist connections.

Pru and Met verified that seemed to still be the case during their two days of recon. The legitimate workers would arrive at 8 A.M. and leave around 5 P.M.

Then at about 11 P.M., other people would arrive. Some of them would take up security positions around the building while the others would continue into the building and stay until 2 or 3 A.M.

It was about 10:45 P.M. when a white van with the print shop logo on the side pulled up to the left front of the building and six men got out and assumed positions around the building; one at each corner, one at the rear, and one in front. Each man was within sight of at least two of the other men at all times. That made it very difficult to take the security people by surprise. A few minutes later, another identical van pulled up in front of the building and from his vantage point, Blue Jay relayed to everyone on the com that five men got out of the van and entered the building along with the security man that was originally in front.

The Team held their positions around the building for twenty minutes when JC's voice came over the com units. "Everything clear in your area, Blue Jay?" JC inquired.

"Clear," Blue Jay said, as he continued to do what he did best, move around and blend into the background without being seen.

"Then by the numbers on my count, ready," JC instructed then counted, "One," and five rounds, fired in unison, took down the five security men.

"Two." The Team moved out of the shadows, checked the downed security men, then formed at the back of the building and waited for Blue Jay.

A few seconds later Blue Jay had joined the Team who was already surveying the building.

"Shades are down so we can't see into the windows to know for sure, but listening gear says no one is in that room," Bean reported to Blue Jay.

"Good," he replied. "We don't have time to deal with alarm systems so we'll pick the lock and if we set off an alarm, it's rock and roll."

Bris took out his lock picks and quickly unlocked the top deadbolt lock, then moved to the doorknob lock and signaled when he had completed his task.

"Ready, sports fans," Blue Jay alerted the Team, then slowly turned the knob and opened the door. When the door was halfway opened, an alarm went off and the element of surprise was gone.

"Shit," Blue Jay exclaimed. "Must be a motion detector. Let's do it," he continued, as he gave the door a hard push and along with Benz and Panda, followed it into the room.

After making sure the room was vacant, they moved into the next room as Bean, Bris, Tic, and Check entered the building. The first three men continued through the first floor of the building, found nothing, and quickly assembled around what looked like a door that led to a basement.

Leaving Check, Tic, and Bris to secure the first floor, the other four prepared to move on to the basement. Blue Jay quickly opened the door that drew immediate gunfire. Panda and Benz quickly threw two flash bang grenades that traveled through the open door and down the steps to the basement. Within a few seconds, two big flashes were followed by big bangs. The sounds from the grenades were still echoing in the cellar when Blue Jay, followed by Bean, descended the stairs with their MP5's firing on full automatic. The grenades followed up with the quick assault were too much for the men in the cellar and they were dispatched quickly.

Blue Jay quickly searched for and found the plates used to print the counterfeit money and then destroyed the press.

"We're missing one of the main men," Bean announced after he checked the last dead body.

"Look around," Blue Jay ordered, not doubting Bean for a second. "Tic," he then yelled up the stairs, "we know the first floor is secure; check the second, we're missing one."

"You got it," Tic replied, as he disappeared from the doorway.

The men in the cellar figured the missing man would probably have been in the area where the printing was going on, so Benz, Panda, Bean, and Blue Jay started searching the large basement very carefully for trap doors, hiding places, and escape routes. Benz was in the far right-hand corner when he noticed a few fresh ink marks on the wall next to a cabinet. Upon closer examination, he discovered they were fingerprints.

Benz moved back from the wall, pointed his weapon in the direction of the cabinet, and using his hand alerted the others about the cabinet. After further inspection of the cabinet, they discovered it was a door that opened to something, but it seemed to be secured on the other side.

"JC, you on?" Blue Jay asked into his com unit.

"I'm on," a voice replied.

"We have the area secured, but one of the main men escaped through a hidden door," Blue Jay reported. "My guess is if we open the door we will find a tunnel to Mexico."

"Want to call it a day?" JC inquired.

"Is the area still quiet?"

"Very," was the one word reply.

"Then let's try something," Blue Jay suggested.

After Blue Jay had relayed his idea, he moved to the cabinet. "No obvious ways to get this fucker open. Well, no matter," he said, as he started pulling on the cabinet then knocking things off the shelf. Panda had discovered a crowbar and started knocking holes in the hidden door. When it got to a point where entry was close, Blue Jay halted the efforts and pulled the men away from the front of the cabinet. "I'd say if a tunnel is behind that door there are bad people with guns at the other end."

The other Team members agreed and prepared their weapons. Standing to the left side of the cabinet Blue Jay gave it a final yank; it swung open and ushered in a volley of rounds. Blue Jay motioned for someone to turn out the lights in the basement and he retrieved night-vision gear. He then lay on the floor and slowly looked into the opening for a quick look. A few seconds later, he said into his com unit, "Just as I thought; a tunnel to Mexico."

"Let's rock," was JC's reply.

"Ready?" Blue Jay asked the others after a few seconds of preparation.

"Ready," was their reply.

Blue Jay then threw a flash bang grenade up the tunnel as far as he could. After it went off, Benz threw another one followed by Panda tossing a smoke grenade. With that completed, Bean and Blue Jay started firing their MP5's and made sounds like they were charging through the tunnel.

As Bean was loading a fresh mag, Blue Jay said, "Spread some of that cocaine around, we are about to leave." While Blue Jay kept up the firing, Bean removed the bag of powder from his inside pocket, and spread it around the area of the tunnel's entrance.

"Looks like a drug thing gone bad to me," Blue Jay approved. "Anything yet, JC?" he then inquired.

"Not yet," was the reply as JC, Pru, and Met searched the area of a house on the Mexican side. "You people call it a day while our luck is still holding," JC ordered.

"May have something at ten o'clock," Met interrupted on the com. Pru and JC immediately turned their scopes to that area and detected a man running down the street. "Think it's him?" Met inquired.

"Can't tell. If he would just look back we could see his face," JC replied.

The man running would have probably made a clean get away, but made one mistake. He looked back to see if he was being pursued.

CHAPTER FOUR

After the Project to take out the counterfeiting operations, the Team was given a week of R&R.

In the past, when they returned to the Barn after R&R, at least a few days would pass before JJ and Mac would call a meeting to present the next Project, but this time after the last member of the Team reported in, they called a meeting.

JJ was again at the front of the room and started by saying, "Sorry we rushed you all into this meeting, men, but we feel this Project has a priority and I am sure you will agree after we present it. Whether you accept it or not is still your decision.

"This time we have a very wealthy man who for some reason started to supply terrorists with weapons. In addition to the usual small arms and explosives, he is trying to acquire more deadly weapons like shoulder held anti-aircraft missiles and biologicals. We don't know the reason for his support of the terrorists. It could be money, but we doubt it. He is already a very wealthy man and with the type of weapons I just mentioned, we feel it's more like a revenge thing. Whatever the reason, we don't care. He is a supplier of weapons that kill innocent people and that's the main reason I decided to form a group like ours, to help prevent the taking of innocent lives."

JJ was getting a little worked up about the subject and the Team was again seeing his strong feelings about what they were all doing.

"I'll now turn over the operational side to Mac," JJ finished.

"Evening, men," Mac started. "If you all approve it, this Project will take us to the Greek Island of Crete. Some of our Projects seem to have us Island hopping in that part of the world. Sardinia, Corsica, and now Crete. I feel wherever they are and whatever it takes, this Team will get the job done."

"Oh, that's good," a voice in the group replied. "Can I sign up for four more in the Corps?"

"Don't worry, men," Blue Jay then added. "I have this new soap that works wonders on getting nicotine stains out of underwear. I used it last time somebody blew smoke up my ass."

A big smile showed up on Mac's face as he said, "Try to give these pecker-heads a compliment and look what happens."

Everyone had a little chuckle before Mac returned to the serious business at hand.

"The code name for this guy will be Dick because that's what he is. I suggested we call him Stiff Dick because we all know a stiff dick has no conscience, but the Board overruled me so it's just plain Dick.

"Dick has his weapons supply centered on Crete. This is only one of his many residences, but he seemed to be spending a lot of time there, probably due to his new interest in terrorism.

"This will work to our advantage. We'll take him out and his warehouse full of goodies at the same time.

"As in the past, we'll get into more detail if you accept the Project. Any questions?" Mac asked, as he finished.

"What kind of security force does Just Plain Dick have?" JC inquired.

"He had a security force of about twenty men, but we have reason to believe he has increased that number and wants to add more. That's another reason we are moving fast on this one," Mac answered.

"I say," Pru started his question, "does the U.S. government know about Just Plain Dick, and if so, why don't they act."

"The answers are, probably and politics," Mac quickly answered.

With no further questions being asked, Mac ended the meeting with, "It's late so we'll meet again late tomorrow morning to get your decision."

As the Team left the meeting room they were unusually quiet, but that seemed to be the norm after a briefing. When they were in deep thought, they got very quiet.

***

By 11 A.M. the following morning, JJ and Mac had gotten a yes from the Team so planning had begun. Additional Intel was given to the Team along with photos, maps, and a layout of the facility on Crete.

JC was quickly going through pictures when he stopped and took a second look at one. "Is this Just Plain Dick?" JC inquired, as he turned it so Mac could see.

"Yeah, that's him," Mac confirmed, as he put the final tacks into a map and pictures he put up on the briefing board at the front of the room. "I'm told that was taken a few years ago in Athens. There should be enough of those to distribute to the Team."

"Gather around here for a little show and tell," Mac requested. "As you all can see, this is a very remote and rugged area. The facility is totally self-contained, only food and a few other necessities are required. See these," he said, as he pointed out large and small light colored objects on the photos. "They are propane tanks. The entire site, including cars and trucks, have been converted to run on propane. Provisions are brought in by truck using the only road in the area or by helicopter if needed."

"The primary objective will be the main man. We feel if he isn't around the operation will collapse.

"Secondary objective, this warehouse. We know he was after biologicals, but don't know how successful in the hunt. If we just take him out, I'm sure the material in the warehouse will be sold off before the operation is shutdown, but he is definitely the main priority."

Mac and JJ worked with the Team for another hour then returned to the main house to put the finishing touches on other parts of the plan.

If possible, the Board tried to locate in the general area where a Project would take place for two reasons. First, the Board didn't feel right sending the Team on dangerous missions while they sat in the safety of their homes back in the States. Second, if on site they could react quicker if the Team needed additional gear or other support if last minute changes to the plan were required.

On two occasions, the Board supplied direct collateral support while maintaining the directive of no contact between Board and Team. For security reasons, JJ and Mac were the only two that knew the completed plans of both Team and Board.

***

A business jet from the U.S. touched down at Hania International Airport on Crete and Dawson taxied it into one of the VIP hangars on the far side on the field. The Board had rented an isolated villa on the Rodopos Peninsula under the pretence of conducting meetings for a joint business venture. This location put them within twenty miles of Just Plain Dick.

The Team had been on the Island since the day before. They landed at an old deserted airfield the British used during World War II. The runway was far from being in good condition, but compared to the airfield on Sardinia that Jockey landed on a few months ago, it was cake.

After checking out the helicopter they would be using for the Project, Jockey was not at all satisfied. JC had called the business jet while they were still en route and expressed Jockey's concerns to JJ. Within an hour, the problem was fixed. Dawson had made a few calls and another copter would be available. He suggested that one be used and the other kept as backup.

So as not to draw too much attention to themselves, it was decided to fly the replacement chopper to the deserted airfield after dark. JC volunteered for the job. Said it was more like the one he used to fly.

***

The following day, Air Jockey and JC checked out both ships in great detail while Blue Jay conducted last minute reviews. It was a go for that night unless they got a bad report about the helicopters.

During a break, Blue Jay went outside, lit up a cigar, and ran through the plan in his head.

'Mac and JC will keep the plane secure until we return. JC will be backup if we have trouble with the primary helicopter. Pru and Met with their .50 caliber rifles will set up about 1,000 yards out in support of the Team and to take out the target if they get a shot. Due to the size of the security force, Benz and Panda

will join the assault group instead of spotting for Pru and Met. Absolute stealth must be maintained to get Tic and Check into the warehouse to set the charges that will be set off remotely. That done the primary target must be taken out or flushed out into the open for the long-range shooters.'

Mac and Air Jockey noticed Blue Jay was in deep thought and alerted JC who stopped what he was doing and walked over to him. "Got another one of those?" he asked, pointing to the cigar.

"Sure," Blue Jay answered, as he went to his inside pocket and produced another cigar.

"What's up?" JC inquired, lighting up the cigar.

"What do you mean?" a puzzled Blue Jay replied.

"Haven't seen you in deep thought like this prior to a mission since you were back in the Corps."

"Just reviewing," Blue Jay answered.

"And?" JC persisted.

"And I have a nagging feeling about something," Blue Jay confessed.

"Is this a, *fuck a mind field,* feeling like you had in Cuba when you changed the plan or is it something else?"

"It's something else. I can't put my finger on it."

"Maybe it's a premonition, better be extra careful," JC advised.

"Well, thank you for that. I never would have thought of it," Blue Jay exploded. "Be extra careful, hmmm, never would have thought of that either. Have to sneak in and if we get discovered, have three to one odds against us. What are you reading, tarot cards now? Madam JC the tarot card reader."

"Just trying to help," JC said with a smile, as Blue Jay walked away, then he added, "And another thing. I noticed you and the Team have been very quiet lately. What's with that?"

"Oh, we've been very quiet?" Blue Jay exploded again, as he walked back to the rundown building at the airfield they were using.

Once he got to the building he stood in the doorway and announced in a loud voice, "Attention, I was just told by the tarot card reader that you ladies have been entirely too quiet lately and he wants to know why. You would think a tarot card reader would already know why, but who am I to argue."

When JC rejoined the other two Mac said with a chuckle, "You always did have a way with the troops."

"It's what I do," JC replied with a smile.

***

It was 11:05 P.M. when Air Jockey notified Blue Jay they were approaching the coordinates of the Landing Zone. They planned to use this site for inserting the Team. It was 2.7 miles from the target area and the Team would move onto the target from there. The pick-up site was set at different coordinates. This was done in case the insertion was observed and an ambush was set up on that LZ. The global positioning devices everyone carried made it easier to do things like that. Prior to that, it was hit or miss, especially at night.

The doors were already opened as the helicopter slowly settled toward the ground. When the wheels touched, the first two men were out followed by the others, and then Jockey and JC were again airborne and headed back to rejoin Mac. First, he would move off a good distance and hover until he knew the Team wasn't dropped into a hot zone and needed evacuation. After hovering for a while, Jockey heard, "It's cold," over his com unit then continued back to the airstrip to wait for the call for pick up.

The Team had quickly moved off the LZ, formed up, and were traveling the 2.7 miles to the objective. One and a half hours later, the Team was all crouched atop a small cliff about 1,100 yards out from a villa where Just Plain Dick was in residence. After checking out the area with night-vision gear, Blue Jay accompanied the long-range shooters as they moved further out onto the cliff ledge to set up in good firing positions. After they selected positions, Benz and Panda gathered material from the area to camouflage the shooter's positions. It wouldn't be needed at night, but during daylight hours, you couldn't just pretend you're out there sunning yourself on a rock. The rest of the Team had performed recon to ensure there were no surprises in the area and reported their findings back to Pru and Met about avenues someone might take to get to their positions.

With the shooters in place, the Team moved out very slowly and deliberately from this point on.

As the Team got close to the villa, Blue Jay whispered into his com unit, "You guys see anything on your thermal imaging?"

"Several of what look like security guards around the villa and several more around the warehouse," Pru reported.

"Okay," Blue Jay replied. *'Why does this guy have that much security on way out in the middle of nowhere?'* he wondered.

The Team was moving through a group of trees when Met's voice came over everyone's com unit. "Picked up a shitload of thermal images to your right front," he advised.

"Security?" Blue Jay inquired.

"Don't think so," Met replied. "It looked more like people walking in a line."

"I say," Pru started, "you don't suppose Just Plain Dick has added some sort of terrorist school to his activities, do you?"

"My thoughts exactly," Blue Jay answered. He then inquired about the direction the people were moving.

"If they continue on, they should pass on your right flank," Met advised.

"Wonderful," Blue Jay replied, as he positioned his men closer together in a circle. If they got into a firefight, all of the friendly fire should be going out with no Team member in the line of fire.

The Team held their position and waited for the people to pass, but they didn't. Instead, they stopped at a campsite they had already set up about 100 feet from the Team's location.

"Well, that isn't good," Blue Jay commented then inquired, "Met, about how many?"

"I make it about fifteen," Met replied.

'Fifteen plus the security force makes thirty-five,' Blue Jay thought. *'The odds are not getting better and we are in a bad position. Better fall back and regroup.'*

Just as Blue Jay was about to give the order, the headlights from an old truck flashed across the fields surrounding the villa as it made its way around the winding roads leading to the villa. The truck passed the Team's position then made an abrupt stop and a man jumped out of the passenger side of the cab. All Team weapons pointed toward the truck anticipating a firefight.

When the man started to yell, the flap on the back of the truck flew up and ten people piled out.

"Easy," Bean whispered over the com. "I think these people are new."

The man did some additional yelling and the ten people took their gear, spread out along the side of the road, and settled in, cutting off the Team's avenue of departure.

"Met, we're ringed," Blue Jay whispered into his com unit. "Notify JC and advise him we cannot stay at our location in daylight. Will wait until things quiet down before attempting to move back to your position."

"Will do," Met replied.

One hour had passed when Blue Jay heard Met's voice on the com. "You on?"

"Yes," was the whispered reply.

"JC advised you to not attempt to move through hostiles. Wants you to wait for the diversion."

"What diversion?" Blue Jay inquired.

"He didn't say," Met relayed.

Blue Jay waited for a moment then whispered, "Okay."

If it were anyone else I would have told them to fuck off, Blue Jay thought, *but since JC said to wait, he must have something good in mind. I hope.*

***

JC and Mac had already prepared a contingency plan in case the Team got into trouble. Without anyone else knowing, the two of them created a plan for every Project, but this was the first time they had to activate one.

Mac and JC disappeared into the jet while Jockey performed a quick preflight on the older helicopter. When Jockey finished, he joined the other two who had already changed into camouflage utilities and were in the process of closing two backpacks they had just filled with assorted goodies. "Guess we're ready for the weapons," JC said to Mac. Both men went to the back of the plane and each returned with an oversized rifle case. After placing each end on the seats of the plane so the cases straddled the passageway, they opened them. Inside each case was an M1 Grande in pristine condition.

"Wow, those old timers are in good condition," Jockey observed. "Are they yours?"

"No, I know a guy. JC and I are sort of partial to the weapon, sooo…" Mac ended the answer, as he positioned the scope and secured it in place.

A few minutes later the two men were ready, had stowed the rifle cases, and were going to leave the plane.

Jockey was waiting at the front of the plane. As JC approached him, he inquired, "I know you are partial to the weapon, but it is an old semi-automatic rifle and I'm sure those bad guys are sporting new automatic weapons."

"That's true," Mac replied, "but we hit what we are aiming at."

"I'm sure," Jockey said, "but there may be too many. Why don't you take the MP5's instead?" he tried to reason.

"These will make the difference," JC replied, as he went into his cartridge belt and produced an eight-round clip for the M1.

Jockey studied the rounds in the clip for a few seconds. "Since the projectiles on the end of the cartridges are more round and blunt instead of longer and to the point, I'd say armor piercing?"

"Very good," JC commended. "And…"

"And that colored ring around the head probably means armor piercing incendiary."

"I'm impressed," JC answered, as he put the clip back into the little pocket on this cartridge belt.

"Yeah," Mac added, "the kid ain't as dumb as he looks."

"Thank you for those kind words, Mac," Jockey responded, as he turned to leave the plane. "Can I make another recommendation? Maybe a bolt action Springfield from World War One for Mac."

Jockey and Mac continued their verbal jousting as they left the plane and walked to the older helicopter. JC was laughing at the one liners and was glad to see things were starting to get back to normal. Mac and the Team were getting entirely too quiet for his liking.

Before the two got into the ship, JC again went over the instructions with Jockey. "Now remember, after we leave, contact JJ and tell him Mac and I are going to try and create a diversion to allow the Team to escape. I would tell him, but he would probably tell me no, followed by a lengthy conversation that would use up time and I would just do it anyway. He'll probably be on the horn, but our radio probably isn't working."

"Got it," Jockey acknowledged.

"Let's do a quick com check right now," JC instructed.

The three men put on their com units and each man walked a short distance away to do the com check. After making sure their com gear worked properly, they received another message. "JC, make sure you bring the old fuck back, okay?"

Mac and JC listened to the message then both looked at Jockey. "You wait until I get back, peckerhead," Mac advised with a smile on his face, as he and JC moved toward the ship.

As instructed, Air Jockey waited until the helicopter was airborne and on its way before he notified JJ.

***

JJ was not happy about the situation, but realized something had to be done. He had just updated the other Board members on the status of the Project and they continued to pore over the photos of the villa, warehouse, and maps of the area. They had already identified the locations of the shooters and the group of trees where the Team were pinned down. With JJ's status update, they were now trying to figure what Mac and JC had in mind for a diversion.

"What exactly did Jockey say?" Foxie inquired, as he and Gil Dunn carefully studied a photo that included the entire complex.

JJ repeated his conversation with Jockey. When he was done, Gil asked, "They didn't tell Jockey how this diversion was going to come about, but did he say anything about other conversation prior to them leaving?"

"Not really," JJ replied, "but Jockey did mention he tried to talk them into taking MP5's instead of the old rifles they had brought along."

"Did he mention what type of rifle," Gil again inquired.

"He said M1's," JJ answered, "but JC told him the ammo would make up the difference."

"What type of ammo?" Foxie then inquired.

"Armor piercing incendiary," JJ replied, as he moved toward the two men going over the photo of the complex.

"You thinking what I'm thinking?" Foxie asked Gil.

"Afraid so," Gil replied, as JJ approached the two men.

CHAPTER FIVE

JC and Mac had landed their ship, were in the area of the villa, and would make contact with the Team before they showed up on Pru or Met's night scopes.

"Anybody on?" JC inquired over his com unit.

After a long pause, an inquiry came over the com units. "I say, is that you?"

"It is," the voice replied, "and I brought a friend."

"Just one?" Met inquired.

"Two Marines should be enough," JC answered.

"What about the diversion?" a whisper over the com inquired.

"You'll know it when you see it. Stay alert," JC replied.

Blue Jay just shook his head as he looked around at the other members of the Team who were all grinning. They knew Mac was the other Marine and that the two of them had probably thought up something wild. Ever since that Project when JC thought up and executed a plan called, *The Floating Simplicity,* the Team wouldn't put anything past JC and Mac.

***

JC and Mac were very slow and deliberate as they moved forward and to the left flank of the two shooters. The sky was

48

starting to get light when the two men decided on positions that gave them a view of the entire complex.

The morning was in that transition phase when it changed from dark to light and everything is sort of gray.

As everything was in the process of changing from dark gray to lighter gray, Met was on the com. "Primary target just came out of the house for a morning cigarette and we have a shot. If we take the shot will it screw up your diversion for the Team's escape?"

"No, but check fire," JC replied, as he looked through his field glasses. "You have a problem coming your way. Looks like a morning security patrol to your right flank."

JC did a quick evaluation. *'Primary target can be taken out, but shooters are in bad position. Could cause diversion before they took the shot to distract the patrol, but that might spook the target.'*

"You are in a dangerous situation. Let the target go, we'll get him another day," JC ordered.

"We are in position to cover the shooters," an unfamiliar voice reported over the com units.

"Identify yourself," JC quickly ordered, not knowing who the voice belonged to.

"It's the Weed Whacker," the voice replied. JJ had given all of the Board members code names, but Mac was still unaware of them, so he decided to put Charles Wilson on the com to make contact.

"They're friends," Mac reassured everyone over the com units, "but keep your heads down if unpleasantness breaks out."

"Is that you, Talley Whacker?" Wilson inquired.

"Maybe," Mac replied. "Are you on, Cuba man?" he then asked, referring to Admiral Fox and his last command prior to retirement.

"I'm on," Foxie replied.

"Are you in position?" Mac asked.

"Yes, only two routes to your shooters and both were covered." When Foxie replied, other voices were heard in the background asking where the long-range shooters were located.

Hearing the questions over the com, each shooter removed a tiny flag from their inside pocket and pushed it up through the camouflage so anyone behind could see it.

"Oh that's funny," Gil Dunn said with a smile. "I see a small British flag on that pile of foliage to the left."

"I see a German flag to the right," Wilson added.

"Don't mean to offend, chaps. Just a little reminder," a British voice informed the Board members.

JC recalculated his options then was back on the com. "Do you still have the shot?" he asked the shooters.

"Affirmative," was the reply.

"Then let's start the dance," JC instructed, as he and Mac took aim.

The primary had just finished his cigarette and stood up for a morning stretch he wouldn't finish as two .50 caliber rounds threw him across the patio and against the house with a thud.

"Target down," was reported over the com. JC and Mac took up the slack in their trigger pull then each squeezed off a round. As two incendiary rounds traveled toward a large propane tank, Mac and JC were acquiring two new smaller propane targets in their scopes. The first two rounds struck the first tank, and as it exploded, a large ball of flame rose into the air as the two men fired their second rounds.

The rounds were working as expected with only one drawback; when you use incendiary rounds, everyone can see where the rounds are coming from. JC and Mac squeezed off a third round then moved to another location before incoming rounds started beating up the area.

SOT 3

***

When the first explosion occurred, the Team held their position until all of the bad people started reacting and running in all directions.

"Let's pretend we belong here," Blue Jay instructed, as the Team got to their feet and moved in the direction of the new people that arrived last night. Not being sure who these men were or where they just came from, the new people moved aside and allowed them to pass.

That worked out well, Blue Jay thought after the Team had moved past the new people.

Benz and Panda were acting as rear guards and had fallen a little behind. The Team had already crossed a path and proceeded up over a small hill by the time the rear guards got to the path. As Benz and Panda started to cross the path, five security men returning from a morning dip in a small pond came running around a bend in the path in response to the continuing explosions and did not hesitate before attacking the two men.

The first man took a wild swing at Benz, but his attack was deflected by Benz's left hand. The same hand then grasped the sleeve of the man. His right hand went to the chest, grabbed a handful of shirt, and with a spinning of the hip, the man went airborne.

While Benz was executing another perfect Uchimata, Panda was being attacked by a left hander who tried to take off his head with a left hook. Panda blocked the attack with his right arm, and then slid the same arm up and around the man's neck, as his left hand grasped the man's shirt. Using the man's forward momentum, Panda spun and slammed his right hip into the man. They both went into the air and when they landed, he was on top.

Panda saw another man coming so he employed a hold down technique that made it feel like the weight went from 150 pounds to a Buick. While Panda maintained control of the man on the ground, he pulled back his left leg and when the charging man was in range, delivered a side kick to the man's groin, putting him out of action.

When Benz completed the throw, he held onto the man's sleeve and while the man was on the ground, delivered a knockout blow to his face. When he completed the move, his back was to the next attacker who planned on making the most out of the opportunity as he quickly moved to the attack until Benz delivered a back kick to his midsection and stopped him in his tracks.

Seeing all of this happening so quickly, the fifth man should have fled, but instead he pulled out a knife. Another reason the man should have fled was the look on Benz's face when he saw the knife. Not being deterred by either reason, the man launched his attack. Benz took a quick step back, blocked the attack with his left hand, and then delivered a punch to the man's chest that drove him back and tumbling to the ground.

With the five men out of commission, Benz and Panda made sure the other was okay. They picked up their weapons and continued their trek across the path and up the hill when another group came from the other direction on the path and started firing their weapons at the two men. This second group really caught the two men by surprise and they had to do some quick scrambling if they were going to make a fight out of it.

As Panda and Benz turned to return fire, the sound of five silenced MP5's opened fire and quickly took out the second group.

"You men all right?" Blue Jay inquired.

"We're good," Benz answered.

"Good, let's mogate," Blue Jay said and the Team once again moved back toward the long-range shooters.

***

After Met and Pru made their shots that took out the main man, they went quiet. If the bad guys couldn't find them, no firefight.

The majority of the security patrol were distracted by the explosions and started to head back toward home base, but the leader of the patrol saw exactly where the two shots came from just prior to the explosions and regrouped the patrol. After he quickly gave new assignments, the patrol was again heading for the cliff and the shooters' positions.

"Security patrol moving toward the cliff," JC alerted, as he surveyed the situations during a brief stop while he and Mac changed positions.

"Roger," was the one word reply on the com, letting him know his message was received.

The ten-man security patrol split in half as they approached the cliff, five to the right and five to the left. As the two groups started to make their way up the slope to where the shooters were positioned, they came under withering fire and within seconds, every man in the patrol was taken down.

The Board members' hearts were beating a lot faster than they normally did when the action was done. "Shooter area secured," Foxie advised on the com.

"We have a gang of asses on our tail," Blue Jay alerted. "Will divert from original destination."

"How many in the gang?" Foxie inquired.

"Must be about thirty," Blue Jay replied.

"Bring them on in," Foxie advised.

"You sure about that?" JC inquired.

"I think we can handle it," Foxie answered.

After a quick conference with Mac about Foxie, JC gave the okay and the Board moved onto the cliff ledge and assumed a perimeter defense per Foxie's instructions.

The Team arrived at their original destination with the thirty-man force in hot pursuit. Being a fast runner in the pursuit group was not a good thing today. When a man from the pursuit group showed up in Met or Pru's scope, they became a fatality.

Realizing his men were dropping, the leader of the group ordered his men back so he could regroup before they assaulted the cliff area.

***

Mac and JC had stopped again and were surveying the situation. JC the cliff area and Mac the building complex.

"I wonder what is in that shed," Mac said out loud.

"What shed?" JC asked, as he watched the cliff area.

"The shed with the security guards that haven't moved since all of this began."

"Maybe they don't want to get involved," JC offered, as he continued watching the cliff area.

About thirty seconds had passed when JC jumped in reaction to an M1 being fired.

"What the fuck are you doing?" JC asked Mac.

"Took a shot at that shed," Mac answered.

"Nothing happened and you gave our position away," JC complained.

"Nothing happened, but all the guards hit the deck when they saw the incendiary round coming in. Then hauled ass away from the shed when nothing happened."

"No shit," JC inquired, as he stopped looking through his field glasses and looked at Mac.

"Maybe we should bring it under fire," Mac suggested.

"Maybe," JC agreed, as he swung his field glasses around to look at the shed.

Seconds later Mac and JC were in the prone position ranging the small shed.

"Range finder says 475," JC relayed to Mac.

"The shed probably isn't full of whatever the guards are afraid of or my first round would have set it off," Mac suggested and JC agreed.

A very short time later, incendiary rounds, two at a time, were heading for and penetrating the shed. Two, four, six rounds penetrated the shed and nothing. JC and Mac would each fire eight rounds before the empty clip ejected signaling it was time to change positions. Eight, ten, twelve, then a huge explosion erupted taking down the warehouse and half of the residence.

"What the fuck was in that shed," an astonished Mac asked.

"I don't know," JC answered, as he grabbed Mac and started pulling him along, leaving the area, "but I hope it's not contagious."

The huge explosion also caught the Team and pursuers by surprise, but the Team reacted quicker and pumped a shitload of rounds into the area where the security force was canceled.

Due to mounting casualties and explosions taking out most of the complex, the pursuers seemed to be a little unsure about what to do next.

Foxie picked up on that fact as he watched them through his field glasses then asked, "Weed Whacker, you want to come here for a minute?"

As Weed Whacker moved close, Foxie started talking and pointing toward where the enemy forces were canceled. A few minutes later, the Sub Thompson was spraying that area with .45 caliber rounds, first from left to right, then from right to left before it stopped.

Foxie's observations were correct. When it seemed to the enemy force the firing had stopped, they decided to call it a day and left the area. The Team and Board held their positions for awhile to make sure the security forces really left the area.

JJ took that time to make sure the Board members all remembered the codenames he assigned them back at the hotel. There wasn't must time to get clever about the codenames, plus he wanted to keep them simple so gave them each a color name. He got all the Board members in a group, explained why they were huddled, then pointed to each man in the group and said in a low voice, "Dunn – Mr. Black, Wilson – Mr. Gray, Dawson – Mr. Brown, Foxie – Mr. Blue, Howard – Mr. Green." With that completed, JJ continued with, "You may think this is stupid, but if anyone on the Team ever gets captured they only know you by a color. The Team members could probably find out your true identities if they wanted, but will not want to know your true identities for that very reason. If you remember, that was the same reasoning when we assigned the Team codenames."

"I sort of like Weed Whacker instead of Mr. Gray." Admiral Fox volunteered with a smile.

"Another one," Wilson replied, "now a swab jockey is on my case. That Talley Whacker Marine started it all."

"Didn't you serve in the Marine Corps?" JJ inquired.

"Yeah," Wilson replied, "but I was in the real Corp. I was an enlisted man."

"Oh, you were an enlisted man," Foxie laughed out loud as the huddle broke.

After JC and Mac performed a survey of the cliff area from their new location, JC was on the Com. "From our location looked like the security force have fallen back to the complex area," he advised.

"We think the same and are ready to move back to position two," Blue Jay relayed.

"Roger," JC acknowledged, already knowing the coordinates for fallback position two.

JC and Mac were waiting for the others when Bris, the point man of the Team, arrived at the coordinates. The duo joined the group and they moved on to the LZ, Jockey, and the two helicopters.

"Jockey, you on?" Blue Jay inquired over the com.

"I'm on."

"Everything okay?" Blue Jay asked.

"Yes, except for these armed men in the area."

"Is he joking?" JJ inquired, as he held his hand over the com unit mic.

"No, that was the password and counter this time out," Blue Jay informed JJ. "If he said everything was okay, we would have made sure you people were secure, and then the Team would have moved onto Jockey's location."

The group was getting very close to the LZ when Bris, still the point man, brought everyone to a halt. Within a few seconds, four Team members moved out to reconnoiterer the LZ. Benz and Panda moved off to the left front with Tic and Check to the right. Due to the terrain, this was completed within minutes.

"Happy to see you all made it back okay," Air Jockey greeted the Board and Team, as they approached the helicopters.

"Thank you," JJ said, as he acknowledged Jockey's words.

The Board got in the newer ship with Air Jockey as pilot while the Team went with JC in the older version.

When both crafts had landed at the airfield, JJ asked all of the Board members to go into the small deserted hangar and JC did the same.

When everyone was inside, JJ started with, "According to our bylaws, the Team and Board are never supposed to meet, but under these circumstances, I guess introductions are in order. By codename only, mind you. I guess the best way to do this is by me. I'll introduce each Board member, and then the Team and Board can mingle. The Team members can introduce themselves so the Board can put a face with the codenames they already know."

With the Board introductions completed, the Team started introducing themselves.

JJ and Mac were very pleased to see the Board and Team members hit it off right from the start.

"I thought they would all hit it off well," JJ relayed to Mac.

"Yeah, that's good to see," Mac answered, "but how did you come up with those codenames for the Board? Couldn't you have been a little more creative?"

"Well, it isn't like I had a lot of time to think about it," JJ replied.

"What you didn't have was me to guide you," Mac stated with a smile.

"Yeah, that must have been it," JJ said, as he faked an agreement. "I see all of the weapons came back this time. Must have been because I was out here to guide you."

"Fuck you," Mac erupted. "You know the reason we did that on the other Projects."

"I don't know anything about it," JJ quipped with a smile.

"Does this happen on a regular basis when they are with the Team?" Gil Dunn, AKA Mr. Black, asked.

"All the time," JC confirmed, "and with the Board?"

"Same," Gil replied.

JJ and Mac noticed things seemed to have gotten very quiet so they looked in the direction of the group and saw the group looking back at them. "Just discussing a few details," JJ quickly announced. "I guess introductions are completed. Maybe we can arrange something more formal at a later date, but for now, I guess the Board and I should get out of these camies."

Fifteen minutes later, JJ and the Board reappeared dressed in civilian clothes carrying their camies and weapons.

"Will you take care of this stuff?" JJ inquired to JC, as he raised his weapon.

"Be glad to," JC replied, as he took custody of his weapons for transport back to the U.S.

The other members of the Team stepped forward and did the same for the others.

Mac went over to Wilson, AKA Mr. Gray, AKA Weed Whacker, and relieved him of the Sub Thompson.

"Now don't drop it or get it dirty," Wilson instructed Mac.

"Oh, I won't," Mac replied. "I'll clean it up for you when I get back to home base." Then he extended his hand to Wilson and as they shook hands Mac said, "Good job."

"Since we are not sure when or if we will be meeting again, the Team would like to express our thanks to the Board, Mac, and JC for getting us out of a very tight spot," Blue Jay started. "I am sure some or all of us would be causalities right now if it wasn't for you people." With that said, Blue Jay, followed by the Team, walked over to the other group, shook hands, and thanked every man.

CHAPTER SIX

t had been one week since their trip to Crete and the Board members were discussing the Team members. Knowing them by codename and background only, the Board members had created a mental image of each man and were surprised in some cases how far off the mental images were from the real person.

JJ and Mac sat quietly and listened as everyone talked about Crete and meeting the Team. Since this was the only place the Board Members could talk about the subject, JJ let them talk for a long time before calling the meeting to order.

"Gentlemen, I guess we should get started," he said and the other members came to order. "The next Project we are going to propose for the Team is a reconnaissance Project. I know reconnaissance sounds less serious than some of our previous Projects, but in fact, it would be extremely dangerous. Mac discovered the problem and did the research so he will present it. Mac," JJ said, as he turned the meeting over to General Mac.

Mac stood, put his briefcase on the table, opened it, removed an aerosol can, and slid the can down to Gil Dunn at the other end of the table. "You may need this, Mr. Black."

Gil picked up the can, read the label, and then said out loud, "Bull Shit Repellent. Why will I need this?" Gil inquired.

"Think in terms of, Don't kill the messenger," Mac replied to Gil who still looked a little puzzled for a few seconds as his brain was multitasking, then realized Mac was probably talking about his former life as DDO.

Mac removed papers from his briefcase then moved to an easel at the front of the room. "Location for this Project would be the Bekaa Valley in Lebanon," Mac announced, as he started the presentation. "Reason, a senior military officer still on active duty has been beating a drum inside the military and intelligence communities about the location of weapons of mass destruction, nuclear WMD's to be exact, with little or no success. Since I have no direct access to classified material, I had to do most of the research in the public media and it was pretty amazing. I'll relate what I found and then maybe someone at the table can give some insight on how things got into their current state."

As Mac paused before continuing his presentation, a popping noise was heard as Gil Dunn removed the top from the can of bullshit repellent.

"This senior officer claimed Saddam wanted the WMD's out of the country prior to any conflict. He asked Syria and Russia for assistance and after a thirty million dollar payment was made, the task was given the go ahead. Units of Spetsnatz, Russian Special Forces, shredded records and moved all WMD's and specified advanced munitions out of Iraq to Syria, then onto the eastern side of the Bekaa Valley in Lebanon.

"All parties involved were a little apprehensive about putting components of the Nuclear WMD's in the valley, but Syria did not want them detected on their soil. It was decided since thousands of Syrian troops were already in Lebanon, particularly in the Bekaa Valley, the weapons would be secure.

"When Syria got tagged for the Prime Minister Rafik Hariri's assassination in Lebanon, the heat was on for them to leave the country. They agreed, but were dragging their feet on the eastern side of the Bekaa Valley. This was probably a good thing because if certain terrorists got their hands on those weapons, we all know what could happen.

"Since Syria is under constant pressure to leave the Bekaa Valley, the matter has to be brought to a head.

"Here is where I feel it gets really amazing," Mac said, as he held up a piece of paper. "I'll now read something I found in the media and I quote, 'There is no question that the Russian effort to remove Iraqi WMD systems was the most successful intelligence operation of the twenty-first century. The Russians were able to move hundreds of tons of chemicals, biological, and nuclear materials without being discovered by CIA satellites or NSA radio listening posts. Unquote," Mac ended, as he shook his head. "In my opinion, there are only two reasons why this could have happened, incompetence or politics. It could have been incompetence, but speaking for myself, I saw CNN report many times about loaded tractor trailers going out the back door when UN inspectors were trying to get into the front and just assumed CIA had a satellite or some other sort of Intel gathering on going in Iraq. But these days who knows.

"If it was due to politics, it was a simple case of Syria and Russia playing catch me, fuck me, while everyone in Washington was wearing blindfolds and saying, I can't find them, I can't find them.

"Before I get too worked up about this, I'll ask a former Deputy Director of Operations at CIA if he can enlighten us on the subject." Mac nodded his head to Gil.

"Would you like the long or short version?" Gil inquired.

"The long version, but hurry up," Mac replied.

"Well, I'll try," Gil started, "but just remember I was DDO at CIA many years ago and am not privy to that type of sensitive information anymore. These days my information comes mostly from the media."

"I thought Spooks at your level were never really out of the business?" Foxie observed.

"Swab jockey," Gil said to Foxie before he started to share information with the group.

"Not sure about the other intelligence agencies, but at CIA it went something like this," Gil started. "Back in 1977, Carter was President and made Admiral Turner CIA Director. Turner thought due to all of the new satellites and other technology, the human factor wasn't that important so they had a RIF, reduction in force, and got rid of a lot of their spies. Now mind you, in some cases, if you got rid of a case officer in the field, you also lost many, many native operatives in that country. Can anyone spell Middle East, Iraq, Iran?

"After that period, Regan and Bush One tried to get things back on track then Clinton showed up.

"The Clinton CIA made the Carter CIA look like a well-oiled machine. I wasn't there, but have heard that the operation's center where intelligence from all over the world came in was dead quiet most of the time. There was even one case where a Case Officer was called back from Iraq because he put in his report back to Langley that he had developed a contingency plan to take out Saddam if it were ever required.

"Per White House orders, the man was recalled back to Langley where two FBI Agents put him under arrest in the hallway at CIA Headquarters for planning the assassination of a world leader. He was eventually released, but not allowed back into the field and resigned some time later.

"Now Bush Two is in and who knows what the hell is going on now. The intelligence community got blamed for 9/11 and I know that caused a mess for the Agency. They had to gear up for a terrorist war and at the same time fight off the politicians. The Agency always had a policy of, 'do not claim your victories' and 'do not admit your defeats'. This policy was in place for many reasons, but puts them at a disadvantage in cases where they are being attacked by assholes. The assholes know CIA will not or cannot respond to accusations, so they have a field day in the media. I think the politicians back when knew the game and bridled in anyone that went too far. Today they panic due to media or public pressure and do something stupid like put in a politician as Director of CIA who brought alone his capital hill staffers. They knew nothing about intelligence work, walked around with a shitty attitude, pissed everybody off when they weren't at a party somewhere, and people at the Agency started resigning. When people like the DDO, his Deputy, and senior analysts at the Agency start resigning, something is not right.

"The politicians were finally shitcanned, but where does that leave things? Who knows?"

"Why didn't the White House act sooner?" an irritated Dawson inquired.

"I have no idea," Gil replied.

"Are the staffers at the White House calling the shots?" an equally irritated Wilson asked.

"Don't know," Gil again replied.

"Being a former DDO, how can you not know?" Dawson asked.

At that point, Gil grabbed the can of bullshit repellent, stood up, and sprayed the shit out of the table area as he repeated, "I don't know!"

Foxie was coughing and laughing at the same time, as he started to say something, but Gil pointed the can at him, gave a little squirt of repellent in his direction, and Foxie changed his mind.

"I thought you would need that," Mac informed Gil, as everyone finally stopped laughing.

"Thanks," Gil said, "where did you get it?"

"I bought a case of the stuff at a novelty shop years ago when I was assigned to the Pentagon," Mac replied. "That was the last can; do I have to explain why?"

"No," Gil answered, echoed by Foxie at almost the same second.

"I guess in summation we can say," a smiling JJ took control of the meeting, "Gil has a pretty good idea of what is going on with the current situation, but has no inside info."

"I thank you," Gil said as he stood, bowed to JJ then sat down again.

"Since a lot of emotions have broken out I think we should take a break before continuing," JJ advised. All agreed and went for coffee or continued their discussions about Crete.

***

The next day, JJ had completed his part of the presentation about the recon Project to the Team and Mac just started his operational overview.

"As JJ said the place for the Project would be in the Bekaa Valley in Lebanon," Mac started. "As you probably already know, the valley sits between two mountains, the Lebanon Mountains on the west side and the Anti-Lebanon Mountains to the East. The valley is crawling with Syrian, Russian, and Iranian military types. It's also where most of the WMD's are stored or buried. In addition to military, the valley is also full of bandits.

"The area we are most interested in is the northeast corner of the valley up by the Syrian border. Syria doesn't want the Nuke WMD's on their soil, but at the same time, they want to keep them close. The objective would be to get in, find the site of the Nuclear WMD's, flashback the coordinates, then leave country.

"I'm really going out on a limb here and you'll probably shitcan the idea," Mac continued, "but since the countries around Lebanon are Syria, Israel, and Iraq, I feel it would be best to enter by sea. Israel has a shitload of security on the border and Syria and Iraq are not good choices for obvious reasons, especially Iraq. If you make your landing up around the Tripoli area, then move east, that would probably be your best route to the northeast part of the valley."

"And on the next Project we'll be going to the Halls of Montezuma," a low voice in the group commented.

Mac, still looking down at his notes said, "Jockey, if that wasn't you I know it was that other shitbird, Panda."

"General Mac, how can you say such a thing," both men said almost in unison.

"I don't know," Mac replied, "probably because it's *true!*"

JC took advantage of the break in the presentation and asked, "How would we get to the Tripoli area?"

"I hear there are a lot of big yachts in the Mediterranean this time of the year," JJ spoke up.

"And out," was JC's second question.

"Undecided, still working on that part," JJ confessed.

"As for being inside Lebanon," Mac continued his presentation, "you are all worldly and know your way around. As for conversing, Arabic is the official language, but French, Armenian, and English are also spoken."

"I say, it's about time English came into play on one of these Projects," Pru said with a smile.

"I think they mean world English, not British," Mac played along.

"Oh, hard cheese," Pru faked disappointment.

SOT 3

Mac quickly glanced over his notes then said, "I think that about does it. If there are no questions, JJ and I will meet with you all again in the morning for the Team's yes or no decision."

There were no additional questions, so Mac adjourned the meeting.

CHAPTER SEVEN

The following morning the meeting was again in session.

"May we have your answer?" JJ inquired.

"The answer is yes," JC replied, "but we need to talk about a few things."

"Fire away," JJ announced, as Mac joined him and stood by a large map of Lebanon they had displayed at the front of the room.

"As we see it, the Team has several ways to get in and out of Lebanon," JC started. "Clandestine, as tourists, hikers, etcetera, or a combination of methods. Since it's not the friendliest part of the world, what type of collateral support is available?"

"Good question," JJ approved, as he moved to the map. "Since in the past the Team chose the clandestine route, the Board addressed those issues, but if you decide to go the tourist or any other way, that can also be arranged. But as you said, *it's not the friendliest part of the world.*

"Let me give you an overview of what we had in mind for support of a clandestine entry," JJ continued. "First, I'm sure you all remember the Iraq Project and the Intel about what apartments would be empty, etcetera?" The Team all acknowledged they did. "Well, that organization is also active it Lebanon and estimates the nukes are hidden on the eastern side in the Bekaa valley

68

across from the Old Cedars of Lebanon at Bcharré in the Chouf Mountains.

"Our home base would be on Cyprus. Thought about loading the Team up on a big yacht, transport you to a position off the coast of Lebanon, and let you make your way ashore in rubber boats or some other type of craft. Then Mr. Blue pointed out Lebanon had a twelve mile limit and might get testy if we violated their waters, so we shitcanned that idea.

"Mac then suggested using a helicopter to transport the Team from Cyprus to the Bcharré. If and when you find the site where the nukes are hidden, you flash us a text message with the coordinates imbedded in it. After you retreat to a safe place, you signal for pick up. The Board and I will be on a yacht sailing in the Mediterranean between Cyprus and Lebanon in case the helicopter has mechanical problems going to or from the Bcharré area.

"Have any thoughts about how we would navigate along the sea route to avoid any boats or ships that could give us away?"

"I think we came up with a good idea for that," JJ answered, very pleased with himself.

***

A helicopter flying very low passed close to a yacht off the coast of Lebanon.

"How do things look ahead?" Air Jockey inquired to Mr. Blue who was monitoring the onboard radar for any type of craft in the path of the helicopter's current course. With the markings of an official Lebanon aircraft on it, there wasn't much chance of them being in trouble if discovered, but better safe than sorry.

Foxie detected what looked like a small fishing boat and advised, "Small craft at your one o'clock. Advise you peel off to port and get some distance."

"Roger," Jockey answered, as he guided the craft to the left and held that course for a while before turning back toward Lebanon.

When the copter crossed the coastline north of Tripoli, Jockey gave one long then two short clicks on the radio mic. That signaled to the yacht that they would not be sending further verbal communications.

With JC in the co-pilot seat constantly checking their location and for any ground identifiers, Jockey set a diagonal course between where they crossed the coast and the Old Cedars at Bcharré. The plan was to position the Team on the western slope of the Chouf Mountains some distance from their destination to keep the helicopter out of sight and sound of the Bekaa Valley. Flying low over almost all rural areas, Jockey wasted no time in getting the Team to their destination. When the helicopter was approximately two miles from the drop-off point, Jockey started slowing down the ship. There was no need to cause unwanted noise trying to stop on a dime to let the Team off.

"You children be careful," JC advised over the com and Jockey also wished them good luck.

The Team acknowledged their good wishes and after a short pause, humming could be heard over the com units followed by *'To the shores of Tripoli.'*

"Mac's never around when you need him," JC remarked with a smile.

"Somebody said he left for Mexico to check out our next Project," Panda advised.

Since Jockey and JC were wearing night-vision gear, there was no danger of colliding with some unseen thing in the darkness as they brought the Team to the exact location of the drop-off. The craft hovered a few feet off the ground as the Team dismounted, moved away, and the ship pulled up and away to the left.

"Everything okay?" JC inquired to the Team, as the ship moved off.

"Okay," was Blue Jay's one-word reply.

The Team formed up and quickly moved a good distance from the landing zone before they stopped to check their coordinates. Once Blue Jay was satisfied, he set the direction and the Team moved out.

Two hours later the Team approached the summit on the mountain and Blue Jay again called the Team to a halt. "If these map coordinates are correct, our objective is on the other side of this ridge," Blue Jay informed the Team over the com units. "We'll keep a low profile as we go over the summit and move into the Old Cedars."

The plan was to move into the trees, blend into the hillside, and observe the area in question the following day. That night the Team would move closer and after positioning the long-range shooters and spotters, the remainder of the Team would take a real close look at the area.

***

A hotshot Israeli pilot flew his jet low over the Mediterranean Sea and picked up speed as it moved closer to its home base in Israel. There was going to be a lot of pissed off people on the phone in the morning due to him breaking the sound barrier that caused a loud boom over their homes at 4 A.M.

***

Blue Jay and the Team were settled into their positions on the eastern slope of the Chouf Mountains when they heard the sound of Triple A and other anti-aircraft fire to the south. When they all looked, it reminded them of the pictures on CNN when Baghdad was under night attack.

***

There wasn't much room for the Israeli pilot to maneuver in the Bekaa Valley, but he did what he could as he kept the pedal to the metal while heading for the target.

At that time in the A.M., he caught the people on duty off-guard, but now they were awake and planes that came up the valley after him would pay a heavy price.

When the jet got close to the Team's location, it released two 500 pound JDAM bombs then immediately banked sharply to the left trying not to enter Syrian airspace. At that speed, the pilot took a lot of G's and his ability to withstand a high G-force without passing out was one of the reasons he was selected. Blacking out at such a low altitude would only spell disaster. As the pilot was fighting the G-force, the two smart bombs exploded on target on the eastern side of the valley. The pilot came very close to passing out, but managed to fight it off and was heading for the Mediterranean Sea a short distance away.

Some of the Team was watching where the bombs struck and others the jet that dropped them when a second jet flew over their location so low that the trees were swaying back and forth in its path. After dropping two more JDAM's, the jet pulled straight up and released chaff flairs as a countermeasure for the surface to air missiles that were stationed in the valley. As the two JDAM's struck in the same place, the pilot discontinued his climb, guided the jet gently over to the right and down to regain speed lost in the climb.

As he performed that maneuver, a third jet made a stealth approach like the second. While the first jet made his attack up the valley, causing the defenders to think other attackers would follow, the second made its low in over the sea attack, and the third jet was hanging out at 40,000 feet, waiting to make its entry.

The third jet had a bad angle of attack, but didn't have much of a choice. When he was lined up on the target, he released two more JDAM's and changed the angle of his dive so the jet would quickly drop behind the relative safety of the Lebanon mountain range. The other pilot performed the same maneuver, but at a slightly different altitude.

As the two jets flew over the valley then dropped down behind the mountain range, they both pooped out a lot of chaff flairs to confuse the SAM's that were coming their way.

This was a good thing for the pilots, but bad for the Team. With all of the confusion, it looked like the Fourth of July. Several of the SAM's followed the chaff flairs, slammed into the cedar trees in the Team's area and one exploded.

"Fuck this," Blue Jay announced into his com, "let's mogate."

The Team moved back over the ridge as Triple A fire continued in the valley. They didn't see anything, but they didn't see the last two coming in either.

Blue Jay paused before he moved over the summit and surveyed the scene through his field glasses.

On the yacht, a focused Foxie monitored all of the communications gear. With explosions being heard in the distance and jets hugging the deck out over the sea, it meant the valley was probably under attack.

The Board knew it was good news when Foxie smiled as he read a flash text message. *'Somebody else knew the exact address and beat us to the account. Send the limo.'*

"I'll notify JC and Jockey to move up the extraction," Foxie said, as he motioned for the other Board members to read the text message.

CHAPTER EIGHT

S ince the last Project was brought to an abrupt halt before it really got started, the Team decided to forgo the usual time off after a Project's completion. Instead, they stayed at the Barn and during the day honed their skills. JC held classes on the latest technical gizmos or whatever else he thought might come in handy on future Projects, and of course the Team members all maintained their excellent physical shape.

The Board always seemed to have something in the queue in the way of Projects, but was in serious discussion about the next one.

Before the Board selected a Project, they would consider three possible candidates, discuss each one, and then vote. When a majority selected one, logistical planning would start and a very high level operational plan would begin. If all the planning seemed to be feasible, JJ and Mac would present it to the Team. As always, the Team had total veto power over every Project.

***

Saturday morning had again rolled around and Blue Jay was going to run an errand in Flemington, a small town north of the Barn's location. He asked JC and the Team if they needed anything and of course, they all did. After he recruited Bean to assist him, they went to the main house to ask Top Kiner and the Ladies if they required anything. The Ladies said no, but Top wanted something for his garden. After explaining and getting nowhere, Top wrote them a note. "Just give this to a person at the store."

"No problem," Bean replied and they departed.

As the two men were getting into Blue Jay's Z28, JJ yelled from the house, "You men going to be away long?"

"We shouldn't be," Blue Jay answered. "Has something come up?" he then inquired.

"No," JJ replied, "just have a little surprise for the Team."

"Okay," Blue Jay said, as he started the Camaro then drove down the long lane to the road.

"Little surprise," Bean grumbled, "they probably are going to send us to *The Halls of Montezuma.*"

"Now don't get your panties in a bind, Nancy Marie. I'm sure it's nothing serious," Blue Jay fired.

"There you go again with that Nancy Marie," Bean replied rather abruptly. "I was just making a little humorous remark."

"It was very little from where I'm sitting," Blue Jay advised.

"So it's going to be that kind of day," Bean observed.

"What do you mean?" Blue Jay asked, as he faked innocence.

"Being critical for one thing," Bean replied then added, "I could do the same and say something about your haircut."

"What about my haircut?" Blue Jay asked, as he looked into the rearview mirror.

"Let's just say if I had a dog with a haircut like yours, I would shave its ass and make it walk on its front paws."

"Oh, that's funny," Blue Jay replied, "old, but funny."

"I'll try to do better," Bean promised.

After a quick stop for gas at Todd's Garage in Stockton the duo were on their way to Flemington.

With all of the other errands completed, Bean and Blue Jay were standing inside The Home Depot studying the note Top had given them. They sort of looked like two monkeys going over plans on how to screw a football when a voice inquired, "I'm Katy, one of the assistant store managers, may I help you?"

Blue Jay and Bean looked up from their note and immediately accepted the young woman's offer. "Yes," Blue Jay said, as he handed her Top's note.

"Can you guide us to someone who can help?" Bean inquired.

"I can help you with this," Katy assured them, as she led them to the gardening department. After the items on Top's list were in the cart, the young women inquired, "Will there be anything else today?"

When they said no she took them to the nearest cashier for checkout and wished them a good day.

"Nice kid," Blue Jay observed.

"Yes, she is," Bean agreed. "After listening to her you could take a lesson and try to improve your personality, if you had one."

"That was better," Blue Jay laughed, "but still not good."

"I'll keep trying," Bean promised.

***

The ride home was far from quiet, but as they pulled into the lane at the Barn, both men went quiet. A new Porsche was parked in the driveway and everyone was inspecting it.

"What's this shit?" Blue Jay wondered out loud.

As the Z28 came to a stop next to where the Team members were standing, Blue Jay inquired, "What's up?"

"Giving us replacement cars," Benz answered.

"We have been waiting for your return," JJ announced, as he and Mac approached the group. "Let's go into the Team meeting room."

When everyone was seated in the Team room, JJ started the brief meeting. "To help maintain the cover of the Barn being a very exclusive Bed and Breakfast for the rich and famous, we feel a change in cars is overdue. Of course, the new cars will be different, but will also have bogus out of state registrations that lead to a dead-end if anyone does an in-depth investigation and we hope no one will do anything to cause an in-depth investigation," JJ said, as he scanned the Team. "We have decided to make the change of cars gradual to give the impression that people checked-out at a normal rate instead of all at once.

"The first car will replace Blue Jay's," JJ continued.

"Teacher's pet," Jockey immediately responded.

"Why me?" Blue Jay protested. "I like my Z28."

JJ would not consider any of Blue Jay's protests as more of the Team members chimed in all busting Blue Jay's chops and having a good time while they were at it.

"Glad to see things are starting to get back to normal," JC said to Mac in a low voice. "The Team has been behaving themselves entirely too long."

"I guess that means I'll be defending myself against verbal assaults again on a daily basis," Mac answered.

"And the downside is…" JC asked.

"Whatever happened to that nice young captain I used to know in the Corps?"

"I think he got recruited for something by a retired general and they are all on their way to hell in a hand basket," JC offered.

"I see someone else is also perking up," Mac observed.

The Team was still having a good time at Blue Jay's expense, as everyone moved outside. Having tried to defend himself with no success, Blue Jay changed tactics. "Yes, it is a nice car," he said and looked through the window of the Porsche, "and I do deserve it," he added to stir up the Team.

"I don't believe he said that," Bris exclaimed, as the Team broke into laughter.

To stir them up a little more, Blue Jay then said, "Mr. Bean, would you like to accompany me for a drive in my new motor?"

"Do I have to?" Bean replied.

"You better go with him," Panda suggested. "He might be tempted to steal it."

"Maybe you're right," Bean agreed, as he opened the door and got onto the passenger seat.

"Better fasten your seatbelt. I've driven in a Porsche with him before," Jockey advised, referring to the Washington, DC Project.

"Look who's talking," Blue Jay responded, referring to another situation where the roles were reversed.

For a parting shot, Blue Jay rolled the new car slowly down the lane, honked the horn twice, and waved out the window to the Team.

The Team responded with a bunch of arms and fingers.

***

It was about 10:50 P.M. when the new car rolled to a stop at a red light in Lambertville, a small town south of the Barn. The duo was talking about the Porsche when the light turned green. Blue Jay proceeded across the intersection and took note of the new Corvette that was doing the same in the opposite direction.

Bean noticed a sudden change in the expression on Blue Jay's face as the two cars passed at the intersection. "What's the matter?" Bean inquired.

"I've seen that face somewhere before," he answered, as his mind raced to remember where. "I know," Blue Jay remarked, as he turned the wheel to the left, and made a U-turn through Cifelli's Sunoco Station, which put him back on Bridge Street heading the other way.

"Who is this guy?" Bean inquired.

"He looked like one of the terrorists that is a little high up on the food chain, but not on the most wanted list," Blue Jay started his reply. "Before 9/11, he was just another turd who took on contracts for anyone, but usually drifted to the bad side."

"You know him?" Bean inquired.

"We had a few run-ins. I think he's a little crazy."

The Corvette was stopped at the red light at the corner of Bridge and Union Street when the Porsche came to a stop behind it.

Blue Jay slid his 9mm and silencer out of their separate holsters and asked Bean to attach the silencer.

"Then you're sure it's him?" Bean asked.

"No," was the reply, "but if it was him, I'm sure he saw me make that U-turn and I want to be prepared."

The light turned green and the Vette immediately turned right onto Union Street squealing the tires as the car made the turn. Blue Jay quickly responded with the same maneuver and both cars headed up the street at a high rate of speed.

The two cars were so intent on each other they failed to notice a Lambertville police patrol car in the corner bank parking lot monitoring traffic. As the two cars sped up the street, the officer was on his radio and started his pursuit.

When the Corvette got to the next available left, it waited until the last possible second then turned.

The Porsche was going too fast to make the turn, so Blue Jay hit the brakes and came to a sliding stop in front of the Standing Room Only pub. By the time the Porsche moved back into the intersection, the Vette had passed Joe Finkle & Son then turned right onto Lambert Land.

The Porsche gave quick pursuit and after the right turn onto Lambert Lane, Bean observed, "This looks like it may go into a dead end."

"If it does be prepared for anything," Blue Jay instructed.

The Porsche weaved through a series of turns and into the Center Club Family Fitness parking lot.

Since the first car had a lead, it was in the lot first and waited. When the second car sped into the lot, it was met with rounds being fired from the Vette.

Blue Jay pressed the accelerator to the floor, the Porsche responded, and flew passed the stopped Corvette, but Blue Jay was quickly running out of the parking lot and had to stop. As part of bringing it to a halt, he performed a 180-degree turn and Bean was immediately hanging out the window returning fire at the other car that again was on the move.

The two cars were making a return trip down Lambert Lane when they both noticed the flashing lights from a police cruiser reflecting off the building ahead.

The police officer from the bank saw the two cars make the left turn and knew the only place they could go was the Center Club parking lot or return to Bridge Street. A second officer had already set up a roadblock at Bridge Street and Lambert Lane, and when the cars didn't appear, the first car started searching.

With the police cruiser around the next turn, both cars looked for a way out then the Vette made a left turn onto a very small lane that led to a dirt lot and old railroad tracks that were no longer in use. The Corvette entered the lot and turned onto the railroad tracks followed by the Porsche. The two cars, driving on the railroad ties, passed Coryell Street and headed south.

The officer at the roadblock was getting an update from the officer doing the search when the Corvette and Porsche still on the railroad tracks flew across Bridge Street and passed the Lambertville Station. People new to the restaurant probably thought it was part of a show, but knew better when they saw the expressions on the faces of the staff.

Past the station, both cars got off the tracks and were again on Lambert Lane south that eventually came to a dead end.

After alerting the bridge police officer about the two cars and to watch for their return, the officer at the roadblock gave chase.

As both cars passed the shit factory, Bean noticed a park service sign and told Blue Jay the road might lead into a park with no exit. He agreed and both men started looking for a way out, but with two cruisers now in pursuit, they couldn't turn back.

Having dropped way off the pursuit pace, the duo looked hard for and finally found a way out. A small canal bridge looked interesting so they crossed it then made an immediate right.

The Vette noticed they had given up the chase, figured out why, and brought his car to a sliding stop.

By the time the Porsche was about to enter the parking lot at Towel Lace, the Vette was crossing the bridge with the police right on his tail. Since the cruisers were bigger, they had a harder time getting across the bridge and the Vette had a lead.

As Blue Jay and Bean entered the parking lot, they almost hit a car that passed in front of them. They swerved to avoid an accident then made for a second exit as the Vette entered the same lot without difficulty and went for the first exit.

West Amwell PD passed the lot and stopped, setting up a roadblock. They heard the radio traffic and joined the police pursuit. When the Vette and Porsche saw the route was blocked, they both turned left onto Route 29/South Main Street.

As they proceeded north, a third Lambertville officer was responding. The flashing lights were rapidly approaching when the Corvette crossed over into the oncoming path of the police cruiser. His scheme was to cause the cruiser to change lanes and crash into the oncoming Porsche.

This was not a good plan for the Vette. This officer had played this game before and wasn't about to give in to some punk in a sports car. The two cars were about to collide when the Vette cut back into his original lane.

"I told you that fucker was crazy," Blue Jay informed Bean.

With four police cars trying to get back into the pursuit, both cars had a good lead as Route 29 merged onto 179 north. As both cars sped past the city limits, they saw oncoming headlights. When the oncoming truck got close enough, the Corvette again decided to play the game and this time was successful. The oncoming vehicle tried to avoid the Vette and that put it in the path of the Porsche. Blue Jay turned the wheel and avoided the collision, but now was heading for a building that housed offices and a drug store. Blue Jay tried to control the car, but on grass, it wasn't easy. The Porsche performed a sliding 90-degree turn and came to rest just short of the building. The engine had stalled and Blue Jay tried to restart.

Bean looked at a sign on the side of the building that was very close and read out loud, "Lou Siwy Account," then inquired, "does this mean you plan to do your taxes early this year?"

"That asshole really pissed me off," Blue Jay announced, as the engine finally started. He pulled forward and away from the building then gunned the engine, spun the car around so it was again heading north, rode down the sidewalk, flew into a small parking lot, and out the exit. When he was done shifting gears, the Porsche was flying.

The Corvette, thinking the other car had crashed, was not in a hurry. The duo flew through Mt. Airy and caught sight of the Vette just outside of Ringoes.

Seeing fast approaching headlights in his rearview mirror, the Corvette picked up the pace, but not too much.

Both cars had merged onto Route 202 north, and when the car behind him passed a gas station, the man in the Vette saw it was the Porsche and the chase was on again.

New Jersey state troopers were aware of the situation in Lambertville, and watched for the vehicles involved. A troop car was heading south on 202 when the two cars passed going in the opposite direction. When the trooper reported clocking them at 105 miles per hour, everyone knew they were probably the two from Lambertville. As the trooper clicked on his flash and headed for the next turnaround to give chase, other state police officers were responding.

The two cars were now approaching Flemington. The Vette knew he wasn't going to get away by outrunning the pursuer, so he decided to try something else. As he approached an intersection, he slowed and made a right turn off Route 202, then a quick left that turned out to be the entrance to The Home Depot. The Vette proceeded into the parking lot and headed straight for The Home Depot building with the Porsche in hot pursuit.

At the last second, the Vette faked a right then turned left causing the left side of the car to go up a little.

Blue Jay was waiting for a move like that and the Porsche ran into Vette's left rear fender causing it to roll over and into the front of The Home Depot store.

When Blue Jay and Bean were sure the man would not be able to get out of the crash before the state police arrived, they decided to leave. Bean was still looking at the crash when he said, "Katy ain't going to be happy about this shit."

"Tell me about it," Blue Jay replied, as he headed the Porsche for the side entrance of the parking lot and escaped through the adjacent housing area.

When Blue Jay and Bean arrived back at the Barn, they told JC what had happened and they decided to conceal the car in one of the smaller buildings until morning.

***

The following morning, JC, Bean, and Blue Jay went to check out the Porsche and were surprised to see the entire Team was already doing that very same thing. Pretending they didn't see the three, the Team started making observations.

"Some people just can't take care of anything," Benz said, as he took a closer look at the dent in the left front fender.

"It's not that he doesn't take care of things, it's just that he always has to be chasing something or other," Bris added.

"Maybe someone should make mention of this at the next Bull Shit Derby," Jockey recommended.

"Are you all finished?" Blue Jay inquired.

"Oh, we didn't see you standing there," Panda offered with fake sincerity.

"Well, the car doesn't look that bad," JC said after he looked it over. "What JJ will say after he hears the tale may be another story."

"We would like to hear that one ourselves and maybe throw in some support on your side," Met offered.

"Come ahead," JC offered, as he moved toward the house.

"I say, Blue Jay," Pru started, as he put his hand on the other man's shoulder. "If JJ gets too upset about the car, we'll just tell him, Hard cheese about the Porsche."

"That would be interesting," Bean remarked and the Team chuckled.

JJ took the news better than expected, especially when he found out whom they were chasing and why.

JJ was on the phone in short notice and had arranged for the car to make sure the police would trace the registration number back to a dead-end.

When JJ returned to the kitchen where the group was all seated, he informed Blue Jay, "I'm afraid you'll have to keep the Z28 for a while longer."

"No problem," Blue Jay said, "I'd rather keep it anyway."

"At least he wouldn't be chasing Corvettes with it," Tic offered.

"I wouldn't be so sure. Maybe one of those Amish horse and buggy rigs are called for," Check added. "Let him start off with one horsepower and work his way up."

JC enjoyed the harassment mostly due to the fact that the Team was getting out of quiet mode.

CHAPTER NINE

The Board finally made a decision about the next Project. Due to the location and the extreme danger the Team would be in, they pondered over it for many hours. Ordinarily, they would not have even considered a Project like this, but they had Intel about the location of a Saudi Prince that was in residence with a warlord for his protection and that prince was a huge financial supporter of Al-Qaida.

U.S. Intel probably had the same information, but was not allowed to act due to political considerations with the Saudis. Even though it was known that the man had given hundreds of thousands in financial aid and continued to support Al-Qaida, he was off limits because he was one of the hundreds that made up the Saudi royal family.

One of the Board members suggested a less wordy reason when he called it, "The bodies for oil program," then added, "I'll bet Teddy Roosevelt is turning in his grave like a high speed lathe."

***

JJ had completed the initial phase of the presentation to the Team and Mac was up. Remembering what JC said about the

Team getting too quiet, and partly because he enjoyed doing it, he decided to stir the troops up a little.

"Well, here we are again talking about another Project, but I'm afraid this one isn't going to be as easy as that last one we sent you ladies on," Mac started. "Air travel, backpacking in the area of historical Tripoli, what more could anyone ask for? You even enjoyed an air show and fireworks display."

JC smiled as the Team started to stir.

Then Mac continued with, "Now most of you have been back at home base resting and soaking up the sun for weeks and you should be ready for a real Project. I say most because some of you insist on chasing terrorists around, at the same time playing hide-and-seek with the police and wrecking a brand-new Porsche.

"Are there any questions at this point?" Mac inquired to the Team who were caught off-guard, but were now up to speed.

"Oh, I don't know," Panda announced. "I sort of have a question about that vacation trip to Tripoli statement!"

That started a round robin that lasted for about fifteen minutes, followed by thirty minutes of serious briefing. Mac brought his presentation to a close with, "If you accept, we feel due to the extreme danger of this Project the operational planning should be entirely up to the Team," Mac stated, as he held up a briefcase full of Intel. "We have covered a lot of information and as usual Top has a great lunch prepared for us, so I'll close with this. JC was concerned about the Team getting entirely too quiet and I hope that explains my opening remarks. In an effort to try and prevent this quiet thing from happening again, we are putting in a big supply of PMS medication for you girls. Lunchtime!" Mac quickly announced then headed for the door followed by the Team.

Laughing and more verbal abuse could be heard as Mac and the Team made their way to the main house. "I guess we're going to have a lunchtime version of the Bull Shit Derby?" JJ suggested to JC.

"Yeah," JC replied, "you can always count on Mac."

***

One week of intense planning had passed when the Team requested JJ and Mac attend a meeting.

"You have given us a real hard one this time," JC told the duo. "We have developed several possible scenarios we would like to run past you. Since northern Pakistan is surrounded by countries like China, India, and Afghanistan, getting in and out will be a task in itself. We have an idea on how to get in that the Board may be able to help us with, but are still working on how to get out."

"Yeah, see if Weed Whacker and the group can help us out with that?" Panda offered.

"Now, now," Air Jockey scolded. "Let's follow protocol, it's Mr. Indigo or is it Purple?"

"You're right," Panda acknowledged, "but I think it's Orange."

Bris made his entry with, "You're both full of shit. It's Mr. Puce."

JC looked at Mac as more entries were being made. He defended himself by saying, "Don't look at me, you're the one that said they were too quiet."

"What was I thinking of?" JC replied then called the meeting back to order.

"Since this warlord is very wealthy, mostly due to his connections with the Saudis, he has a well trained and equipped force. The prince stays at the main compound when in country and the security force is on full alert 24/7 during his stay. Our

Team is too small to take on a force that size, especially with them sitting in defense and the Team is too large to make a stealthy entry. With that in mind, we decided on a one-man entry and will employ Blue Jay's special skills with the Team in close support."

***

The Board had arranged a sale of petroleum products to a company in Pakistan. Since the deal was made through one of the bogus companies they had set up for this type of activity, they had total control over the delivery of the petroleum products, among other things.

***

An old C-130 had landed at a small Pakistani airport not far from their objective. Air Jockey had the large aircraft stopped per tower instructions prior to taxiing, as JC quickly checked out the area to make sure it was all clear. When satisfied, he notified the acting crew chief that it looked good for the Team to go.

When Mac heard the words over his com unit, he said, "Well, ladies, it isn't Tripoli, but it will have to do." Then added, "Be careful," as he opened the door to discharge the passengers.

The Team was out of the plane in no time, moved quickly into the total darkness, and was gone. No vehicles were used for getting to the site; they would draw too much attention and with the compound only 3.2 miles from the airport, the Team planned to hoof it.

It was 12:23 A.M. and the Team was set up about half a mile from the compound. From this point, Blue Jay would make his way to the compound, gain access, and then seek out the target.

After a quick review of the contingency plans, Blue Jay was gone.

It was no problem for him to get into the compound for the man, who in addition to his training had natural abilities to do things like that. He made his way through the huge complex and looked for a place where a prince may be housed and decided it must be a two-story building at the far end of the compound. Once there, he made entry and searched through the corridors until he discovered two bodyguards standing outside a suite of rooms.

'Must be it,' Blue Jay thought to himself and made sure the silencer on his weapon was tight. Blue Jay stayed in the shadows and planned his approach to the two men by the door. He could get to a point closer to them, but after that, it was cowboy time.

Blue Jay crept to a position close to the two men then before he was discovered, broke into a run in their direction. Feeling they were at a location of relative safety, the two men had let their guard down, a mistake they would not get a chance to correct.

As he approached at a run from their right side, the man closest to Blue Jay didn't have much time to react before two rounds entered his head and he fell to the floor followed by the other bodyguard. Blue Jay kept moving, grabbed the handle on the door, gave it a turn, and he was in the suite of rooms. Two men were standing in the middle of the room looking at papers. The shorter one reacted quickly and pushed the other man so he was between himself and the intruder. Blue Jay took out the man in his path then the Prince, but not until he had pushed the button on what looked like a locket hanging around his neck. Pushing that button set off a silent alarm in the security room and men were already responding to the suite of rooms. Blue Jay checked to make sure the Prince was dead, then quickly moved back to the corridor and started his escape. Hearing a bunch of footsteps coming from the direction he was heading, Blue Jay reversed course.

The warlords' men yelled for him to stop, but Blue Jay saw another corridor leading off to the left and figured he could get to it before the pursuing men opened fire. He made the turn before they opened fire, but was greeted by another ten men with weapons at the ready. They didn't fire, but instead motioned for him to raise his hands.

'Too many,' he thought and complied.

After being disarmed, searched, and his hands bound, Blue Jay was escorted to where the warlord was waiting. The large room looked like some sort of training hall with wooden floors and several huge windows.

After he told all but three of the men to leave and to search the grounds for any other intruders, he said, "You have destroyed a large portion of my income." Referring to the dead prince, "I'm not saying I'll miss him, but money is money."

***

As the warlord spoke, he was spotted by Benz who was keeping the compound under surveillance. "Not good," Benz said in a low voice. "They have Blue Jay." Benz then directed them to the location and the others quickly zoomed in on the scene.

***

"My Saudi friends are not going to be happy about this. To try and make amends, I'll have to think of something special for you," the warlord informed Blue Jay, as he turned and walked over to the sword rack that held a collection of Samurai swords and removed his favorite.

He then instructed two of the men watching the prisoner to do the same and to get a third for the man that kept watch over Blue Jay.

"These Samurai swords are excellent weapons," the warlord informed Blue Jay, as he removed his from its scabbard and admired the blade. "The strength of the sword the crusaders used plus the sharp edge of the middle east defenders blade, as you will soon discover," he added, then instructed the other three men to remove the swords from their scabbards and take up positions to the left, right, and behind Blue Jay.

***

With the exception of the long-range shooters, the Team was on the way to execute one of the contingency plans when Pru informed Bean what he and Met saw in their scopes.

"Want us to take out the leader?" Pru asked.

"Can you get all four without hitting Blue Jay?" Bean inquired.

"At these angles it would be rough, plus a round may pass through a target and hit Blue Jay," Pru replied.

"Hold fire and relay a second by second description of what is happening," Bean ordered.

***

The warlord had just completed his instructions to the other three men when Blue Jay inquired, "Do those toad stickers have some kind of honorable heritage that go with them or are they just something used to hack with?"

"They have a long history of honor," the warlord quickly replied.

"Oh yeah," Blue Jay replied, "I wonder if four of them ever surrounded an unarmed, tied up man and hacked him to death? I think that would be a dishonorable act."

The statement pissed off the warlord, but he kept his cool, walked over to the sword rack, and returned with another sword. He then slid the sword, still in its scabbard, under the belt on Blue Jay's left side until the hilt on the sword stopped its progress. The warlord then stepped back and said, "Now you are not an unarmed man," and he and the others laughed.

Blue Jay then held out his tied hands, but the warlord said, "Not a chance."

***

When Pru relayed about the sword being put under Blue Jay's belt, Bean said, "That isn't good, things are probably going to get ugly real fast."

"Should he take out the leader?" Pru inquired.

"No," Bean replied.

"How about at the last possible second," Met then inquired.

"No," he replied, "you might hit Blue Jay."

"I say," Pru started to speak, but was cut off by Bean asking, "What part of no don't you understand?"

"Roger," was the reply.

***

Blue Jay seemed to accept his fate as the warlord slowly raised his sword over his head in preparation to deliver the first blow.

As the sword reached its highest point prior to slashing down, Blue Jay, with his hands still bound, grabbed the handle of the sword with his right hand and pulled it out of its scabbard. As the tip of the blade cleared the end of the scabbard, he gave the handle a downward twist and continued the arch movement until he delivered a strike to the warlord's midsection.

Without hesitation he then turned 180-degrees to his left, raised the sword overhead as he turned, and when the turn was completed, he brought the sword down delivering a slashing blow to the man standing behind him.

Both attacks happened within a split second taking the other two men by complete surprise.

Before they could react, Blue Jay continued the attack, turned slightly to his right, twisted the sword handle until the sharp edge was facing upward, and performed the same attack in reverse as he swung the sword in an upward motion.

As the third man fell backward, the fourth attacked. Blue Jay spun the handle of the sword so the thicker backside was facing upward as he prepared to block the oncoming attack.

As the fourth man's sword struck Blue Jay's, he employed a bind, something usually seen in European Fencing. While he maintained the pressure on his opponent's sword, he rotated his until the tip pointed toward his attacker's midsection, then rode the blade of the other sword to the last attack.

With all four men disabled, Blue Jay spun the sword until the point faced downward, forced it into the wooden floor, and then cut the rope binding his hands.

That completed, he freed the sword from the floor's grip, turned the sword until the left side of the blade was facing the floor, quickly swung the blade to his right, and stopped the movement abruptly causing any blood residue on the blade to fly off.

He then in one continuous movement moved the sword to his front, gave a downward dip to the blade, then started to rotate the point of the blade back toward the scabbard at the same time bringing his right arm back toward himself. As the point completed a 180-degree rotation, it was in a direct line with the entrance to the scabbard. The sword was allowed to enter and continue its journey until the guard on the sword slammed against the entrance of the scabbard.

Having just executed a classic quick draw attack, then holstering of the sword, the wounded warlord watched Blue Jay's every move.

Facing the warlord with his left hand still holding the sword, Blue Jay gave a slight bow and said, "Thank you for giving me the opportunity to defend myself. Your wounds should not be fatal."

The warlord acknowledged his words with a head nod. Blue Jay quickly gathered up his weapons, turned, and headed for the big double doors that led to the corridor.

***

"I say, I'm not sure what I just saw," Pru relayed to Bean, "but Blue Jay just escaped."

"I told you it was going to get ugly," Bean advised. "Now you two concentrate on the main entrance and support the diversion when it starts."

"Roger," the two shooters acknowledged.

***

After the three men gained access to the huge compound, Bean positioned Benz and Panda so they could supply cover fire if a hasty retreat were required, then entered the building.

Blue Jay was making his way through the large corridors when security guards en route for the changing of the guard appeared from around the corner. Blue Jay immediately turned and ran for the stairway he had just passed, but the guards reacted quickly and gunfire erupted, forcing Blue Jay to stop just short of the stairway. Hugging the wall behind a pillar, he returned fire until his MP5 got a serious jam.

The security force sensed their adversary had a problem and advanced on his position until another MP5 opened fire taking two of the guards down as the remaining three dove for cover.

Expecting their new adversary to seek cover after the initial burst of fire, the three security men decided to return fire, but were surprised. When they came out to return fire, Bean was still standing in the middle of the hall and another burst from his MP5 took out another guard. With rounds flying all around him, he took out number four. The fifth thought it was time to get reinforcements and immediately departed.

"Well, if it isn't the infamous sword fighter Toshio Baboonie," Bean said to Blue Jay who was still clearing the jam in his MP5. "Were you waiting for them to run out of ammo so you could challenge them to a sword fight?" Bean then inquired.

"Something like that," Blue Jay fired back then inquired, "What was that stunt you just pulled, are you some kind of new superhero?" he inquired.

When he cleared the jam and chambered a round, he motioned for them to move out.

As the duo started to move down the corridor, Blue Jay sang, "It's a bird, it's a plane, its Super Stupid."

"I'm not coming in after your ass next time," Bean announced.

"Yes, you will," Blue Jay contradicted.

"No, I won't," Bean disagreed.

The diversion was already in progress as Bean and Blue Jay made their way across the huge compound. Following the contingency plan, they moved to the right corner of the compound where they met Benz and Panda.

"Remind me not to go in after Toshio Baboonie next time," Bean requested over the com.

"Yeah, keep Super Stupid out here with you," Blue Jay added.

Benz and Panda heard their comments over the com after the firefight inside the building, but were sure a laugh or two would be had in the telling of the entire story.

Bris, Tic, and Check with support from the long-range shooters were doing a good job with the diversion, but were under heavy fire until Blue Jay, Bean, Benz, and Panda slammed into the right flank of the warlord's forces. With rounds now coming in from two directions, the security force started to fall back to regroup. As they did, both groups tossed several smoke grenades to cover their hasty departure.

Bris was acting as rear guard as his group made their move when four of the opposition charged through the smoke searching for the enemy.

Bris downed the first two with a burst from his MP5, but that emptied the magazine. Knowing he would not have time to reload, he fell to his left side at the same time drawing his 9mm Beretta. With his body was still bouncing from the fall to the ground, he pointed his weapon toward the remaining two. There was no time for aim and fire so he twisted the weapon to the left and started firing. As he moved the weapon from right to left, he knocked down the remaining two.

Hearing the gunfire, Tic and Check immediately returned to the area, saw Bris on the ground, and thought the worst.

While Tic stood guard, Check went down close to Bris and asked, "You hit?"

"No," was the reply.

Hearing he was okay, Check and Tic grabbed him, yanked him to his feet, and the three continued their escape.

Thinking the smoke would be used to cover an attack, the enemy force rapidly fired into the empty smoke until they realized no attack or return fire was coming. When they, too, had stopped firing, dead silence fell over the compound.

After they collected the long-range shooters, the Team headed back to the airport and their ride home.

**

The airport was small, but the two runways were extended years ago to accommodate large aircraft incase war broke out with India.

The Team was in place on the airfield when Air Jockey started to taxi the C-130 for takeoff. Plan was for the Team to wait out of sight at the end of the runway. When the C-130 came to a stop prior to take-off, the Team would board. If the plane didn't have to stop prior to take-off, Jockey would make up a reason to stop for a few minutes while the Team got onboard.

The C-130 had taxied halfway down the field when they were ordered to stop the aircraft and wait for additional instructions. JC relayed the information to Blue Jay and everyone went into hold mode.

A few minutes later a police car was racing their way followed by a truck full of Pakistani soldiers and the plane was instructed to standby for inspection.

Wanting to act very cooperative, Mac lowered the rear ramp that would allow access to the plane and Air Jockey came down to greet them and ask what the problem was.

The police car rolled to a stop by the ramp followed by the truck. The soldiers got out of the truck and surrounded the plane while four police officers walked up the ramp and into the plane.

"What's the problem, officer?" Jockey inquired.

"There has been some trouble in the area and we are checking all departing aircraft," the officer answered, as he looked around the plane. The other three officers searched the plane more thoroughly and when they found nothing returned to the ramp.

"You may continue," the officer told Jockey then turned and the four men walked down the ramp. A few commands were given and the soldiers got back onto the truck and both vehicles headed back toward the terminal building.

"Talk about timing," Jockey said to Mac. "If they stopped us just prior to take-off the shit would have hit the fan."

Mac didn't say anything, but shook his head in agreement, as he raised the ramp.

When Air Jockey returned to the flight deck, the plane resumed its taxi. JC alerted the Team about the situation and they moved into position. Mac had the door open when the plane stopped and a few seconds later the first Team member was onboard followed by the remainder. Bean and Blue Jay were the last two to board and the door was slammed shut.

When the tower gave permission for departure, Jockey wasted no time in getting the plane onto the runway. With the plane in position, Air Jockey pushed the throttles forward, the big plane started down the runway, and when it reached take-off speed, he eased it into the air.

After they were airborne, everyone started to relax a little.

"Blue Jay, where did you get that?" Mac asked, as he pointed to the sword.

"From now on he will be known as that infamous sword fighter, Toshio Baboonie," Bean interjected, "but you can call him Baboonie for short."

"It's a long story, Mac," Blue Jay answered.

"Well, I have no place to go for a while," Mac replied.

"Yeah, I would like to hear it as well," Bean again spoke. "Would really like to know how you got that warlord to put that sword under your belt."

As Blue Jay told his story, the plane headed south to the sea, out of Pakistan, and back to the Barn.

CHAPTER TEN

Gil Dunn was at home working in the den when the phone on his private line rang. Not many people knew that number so Gil quickly picked up. "Hello?"

"Gil, glad I caught you in," the familiar voice of Di Flippi replied. "Just checking in with you about our little day trip tomorrow."

"To tell you the truth I forgot all about it," Dunn replied, not knowing what Di was talking about.

"I checked the weather and it's supposed to be a nice day at Sharpsburg. Glad it wouldn't be raining. I want to take my time to inspect the area to try and figure out why the Union General kept attacking across that bridge instead of searching for another crossing."

Since he was also interested in Civil War history, Gil was now aware of what Di was talking about, but the why was still a mystery. "I've always wondered about that myself," Gil said, going along with the conversation.

"I'm leaving home very early tomorrow morning," Di informed Gil. "Want to stop by and visit with John's widow? Getty oil probably has more money, but she is the richest bitch in that burg." Di Flippi laughed.

"John left her well off to start with and over the years she became quite the businesswoman. I'll bet she is worth plenty," Gil agreed.

"Little woman, but big up top," Di observed, as he seemed to be remembering the past.

"I'm sure John would not appreciate that comment," Gil scolded.

"Just an observation," Di quickly replied, "but maybe I shouldn't be talking about John's wife like that. Well, I better hit the sack, early day tomorrow."

"Okay, see you tomorrow," Gil replied then hung up the phone.

'Here we go again with this shit,' Gil thought, as he started to study the notes he had taken during the conversation. *'John's widow are the alert words and the following sentence tells me the location. Getty oil probably has more money, but she is the richest bitch in that burg. First and last words Getty and burg. Talked about the Civil War must be Gettysburg. Next sentence little woman, but big up top. Little Top. Gettysburg at Little Round Top. John's wife end of message.'* After Gil figured out the real location, he sat back in his chair and reflected on the conversation with Di. *'Has to be something very important for him to request a meeting with such short notice. Could be about most anything. After that rescue of two of the retired CIA Agents on Corsica, it would be pretty hard to believe that Di was still unaware of my involvement with some sort of anti-terrorist group outside the government. Well, whatever it is I'll find out tomorrow. John's widow sounded inviting,* his thoughts wondered. *Very rich with big boobs. Too bad she doesn't exist.'* Gil smiled then returned to the work on his desk.

***

Gil was already parked in the lot at Little Round Top when Di Flippi drove up and parked a few spaces away. Gil got out of his car and walked to greet him. "Good to see you again."

"Good to see you as well," Di replied.

After a brief conversation about the battle at Little Round Top, the two men surveyed the area and eventually wandered to the area where the Maine Regiment had been set up in defense during the battle.

After he looked around to ensure they were alone, Gil said, "With all of these coded messages and everything maybe we should have a sign and countersign when we meet," Gil suggested. "For instance, eat shit and countersign could be howl at the moon."

Di Flippi looked at Gil and said, "Eat shit."

Gil replied, "Howl at the moon."

"That wasn't a sign," Di corrected, "it was a request."

The two men chuckled at the exchange and then the conversation changed to the reason for the meeting.

"We have what could be called a huge dilemma," Di Flippi started. "I know you are already aware of what I am about to say, but if the word leaked out it came from intelligence sources; that wouldn't be good."

"Understand," Gil acknowledged.

"As you know I'm now working in the anti-terrorist area," Di started. "We have developed a source that functions inside the terrorists' network. You don't need to know the who, how or why, but something we found out through the source you do need to know. I'm telling you this for two reasons. One, Jar Head and Doggie are again in jeopardy. Two, the group that rescued them on Corsica are on a hit list. Apparently, a group of individuals has been putting a dent in the financial support side of the terrorists' network and they want to know who they are and destroy them.

Our source, in order to protect their own ass, pointed to the group that rescued the two agents on Corsica and suggested those two agents be found, interrogated, and if it looked like the group that rescued them could be the one they are looking for, destroy it."

"They must think Jar Head and Doggie know the group that rescued them," Gil surmised.

"They do know Blue Jay and Bean," Di Flippi replied, knowing the duo and Gil had to be part of a group from the private sector that had declared war on the terrorists.

"What are you folks doing about it?" Gil asked.

"Higher ups feel if we put a wall of security around the two men it will compromise our source inside the terrorist network," Di answered.

"And I guess you aren't going to tell Jar Head and Doggie either?"

"No, and for the same reason," Di again answered. "You know the drill."

"Yeah, I had to make a few rough decisions when I was DDO," Dunn admitted.

"Thus the dilemma," Di Flippi continued. "If Jar Head and Doggie are found by the terrorists, the end result will be they are dead men. If drugs are used and they give the two names they know, it may lead to the bigger organization. If Blue Jay, Bean, and the group intervene, it will probably blow their covers, destroy the group, and will call for an investigation inside the Agency."

"Dilemma with a capital D," Gil added then continued. "How long have we known each other?"

"Counting fifteen years at the Agency, well over twenty," Di answered.

"When are you planning to retire?" Gil then asked.

"Maybe next year. Why the questions" Di asked.

"Because we have been dancing around a subject ever since you called me about that problem after 9/11 and I think it's time for me to bring you up to date. Especially since you have put yourself in situations that could have meant serious trouble for you in many ways," Gil answered, and then started to tell Di about the Team and Board at a high functional level only. Next year he could tell Di the whole story if he became a member of the Board.

Gil kept talking while staying on the move. It didn't take long to bring Di up to speed. For one thing, he was on the edge of some of the Projects plus he was a quick study.

When Gil had him up to speed, Di asked, "What are you going to do?"

"Good question," Dunn replied. "For one thing, the Team will probably have to get involved and before that happens, the Board will have to know why, but first I have to come up with a way to protect the source; that would be you."

"Appreciate that," Di replied.

"Let's walk around the battlefields while we give this some thought," Dunn suggested.

"Good idea," Di agreed.

The two men didn't have much to say as they walked. Di Flippi knew from their days at the Agency when Gil was this quiet he was usually in very deep thought. After they had walked for a long time, Gil said out loud, "Yeah, that might work."

"Come up with something?" Di inquired.

"Believe I have," Dunn answered, as he motioned toward a deserted bench.

As both men took a seat, Gil removed a notebook from his inside pocket, opened it, and began to write. After filling two pages, he handed it to Di to read. When Di Flippi finished reading, he motioned for Gil's pen and wrote a few questions in the book. This back and forth process went on until both men were satisfied with the initial plan. Dunn would fine tune it, but it would not change a great deal. If it did, Di Flippi and he would have to meet again.

"We have to find a place to burn these," Gil said, as he removed pages from the notebook.

As both stood up, Gil realized they were at cemetery ridge and said, "Holy shit, how did we get all of the way over here?"

"You walk a lot when you're in deep thought," Di observed.

"Well, screw the walk back," Gil advised, as he turned and started walking toward the town of Gettysburg.

As they walked past a small building, they read a sign advertising sightseeing tours and decided to take a bus tour back to Little Round Top.

After the two men explained to the tour guide why they were leaving the tour, they collected their cars and headed for a restaurant on the edge of town close to cemetery ridge.

After the two enjoyed a long dinner, they started their return trip home. The first two hours of Gil's five-hour drive were filled with good memories of years past, but then his thought process turned to the business at hand and fine tuning his plan. *'It was a simple plan if Di was able to get him a crucial piece of information. If not, it was onto Plan B, whatever that was.'*

***

The next day, Gil requested JJ call a meeting of the Board and by 2 P.M. the Board was in session.

"I get a bad feeling when someone requests a special meeting," JJ told Gil.

"Am afraid your feelings are right on the mark," Dunn replied and the other Board members become more focused on what Gil was about to say.

"I have an independent source in France that I have maintained for many years," Dunn started. "During the Project on Corsica, that source made arrangements for news releases and transportation, among other things. That person shares information with me from time to time, and being aware I was involved with that Corsica rescue operation, shared some important Intel with me.

"The good news is we seem to be putting a dent into the terrorist's network, especially the financial support department. The bad news is, they are pissed and are hunting for whoever is responsible.

"Being totally in the dark and drawing for straws, they started taking a strong look at the group that pulled off that rescue on Corsica, especially since informed sources told the newspapers it was not an elite French Intel unit as originally reported."

"So they're looking for us," Foxie stated.

"It gets better," Gil replied. "Apparently, one of the bad people reasoned if they got a chance to interrogate the two men, Jar Head and Doggie, it may lead to the group that rescued them, the group being the Team and us. At that point, they would be in a position to evaluate if the group is the same one they are looking for."

As Gil paused a little to let the words sink in, he thought, *'It's basically a true statement, just a little bent here and there.'*

"Gil, you certainly know how to fuck up a perfectly good day," Mac advised.

"Do we have any kind of timeframe?" Foxie inquired.

"Nothing definite, but it gets even better," Gil replied. "According to my source, Al-Qaida has been training special groups for situations like this and the first group was ready for their first mission."

"Before I say anything, does it get any better?" JJ inquired.

"No, that's about it," Dunn finished.

"First of all, I don't think we require a vote on this Project, it's obvious everything else goes on hold and all time will be spent on this one," JJ stated, as he looked around the table and all agreed. "You said nothing definite on a timeframe, so we should assume they are not sitting around."

"I feel we should plan for both defensive and offensive actions for this Project," Admiral Fox suggested then asked, "What do you think, General Mac?"

"I agree and favor offensive action," Mac replied. "If we go into defensive mode, we may not know when or where they will strike Jar Head, Doggie or even the Team or Board. Gil," Mac continued, "can your source find out where or at least the general area of where this first group of Al-Qaida people is located? We will require that if we decide to go on the offensive."

"Already have him working on it," Gil assured Mac and the other Board members. *'That was almost true,'* Gil thought. *'It is being looked into, but the him is Di Flippi and not his source in France.'* When Gil and Di passed the notebook back and forth, Dunn asked him to find the location of the first group's training camp.

Two days of planning had passed and the Board was ready to pass their plan over to the Team for consideration. Dunn's source had discovered the location and he passed it onto the Board. Transportation and logistics were still being worked out, but the operational plan could go forward.

JJ and Mac would call a meeting for the following day and present everything to the Team.

CHAPTER ELEVEN

The following day, JJ informed the Team about the situation and why the Board decided on an offensive rather than defensive solution. With no questions asked, the operational overview started.

"Morning, men," Mac started and the Team acknowledged his greeting. "As JJ said, this will be an offensive Project, but didn't say where. It will be in Chile," Mac stated, as he looked for a misplaced sheet of paper.

"Chile?" a voice inquired.

"Yes," Mac confirmed. "You know, in South America, Eastern Island is off the coast. I'm sure you all have heard about that island."

"It's where the Easter Bunny lives," Panda announced.

"It's where the Easter Bunny lives," Mac echoed the words.

"No, it's where they make all of the Easter baskets," Air Jockey corrected Panda.

"It's where they make all of the Easter baskets," Mac again echoed the words.

"Well, you're both right," Mac answered, "but in addition to that, it's mostly known for the huge stone sculptures on the island and no one can figure out how they were made or who moved them to the coastline. Of course, they haven't given these two a shot at the puzzle," Mac announced, as he pointed to Jockey and Panda.

"It was the Easter Bunny's older brother, Big Bunny!" Panda said.

"And he carried them in a big basket!" Jockey added.

Mac just looked at JC as everyone broke into laughter about the exchange.

"Well, at least they aren't quiet," JC defended.

The Team got quiet after the humorous exchange then focused on what Mac was saying.

"This Project will differ from ones in the past where we went into accomplish an objective and only engaged the enemy if we needed to. This Project will be an offensive combat Project similar to a combat patrol in the military where you try to inflict as many causalities as possible on the enemy.

"The Al-Qaida people in that training camp will be looking for us and that is reason enough to take them out. Another reason would be, if left unchecked, those people in the future would inflict serious injury or kill innocent people and that's an even better reason to take them out."

After Mac had completed the presentation, the Team needed no additional time to decide and voted yes on the Offensive Project and planning began immediately.

Since the Team already agreed to accept the Project, Mac started to go into more detail about the operational side.

"We have a few options available in the transportation area. By air, I'm sure Jockey would have no problem eluding detection, getting in and out of the area. The other possibility is by sea."

"Can you spell amphibious landing?" a voice in the group inquired.

"That could be ladies," Mac quipped. "Unfortunately, the landing would be made without the use of an Amtrac so you girls might get a little damp."

"First the shores of Tripoli, now this," Panda grumbled. "I want a transfer."

"Maybe we should sing Mac the Marine Corps Hymn?" Jockey suggested, hoping everyone remembered Blue Jay's version.

"You mean The Halls of Montezuma?" Panda inquired, playing the part of the straight man.

"No, the other Marine Corps Hymn," Jockey corrected. As he started singing, the others joined in. "Himmm, Himmm, Fuck Himmm."

"Very funny, very funny," Mac scolded with a smile on his face then continued with the briefing.

When he had exhausted all of the information, he said, "That is all of the information I have at present. Tomorrow morning we will meet again with the Board and by afternoon you will have all of the additional information and Intel they have gathered. With that said, I'll let you get started on your detailed planning."

***

The following morning, the planning continued at The Barn. On past Projects, entering and exiting another country using aircraft of different types was always successful, but this time the Team agreed it would be better to fly into an airport in southern Peru then use a boat to transport them to the area around Afica along the coast on the northern tip of Chile. JC informed JJ and Mac about their idea, and they in turn passed it onto the Board. If they agreed, the Board would start planning and getting the logistical support into place.

***

One week had passed since Dunn had dropped the bombshell on the Board and they were attending their last meeting prior to the operational phase of the Project.

Not being able to get an idea about a timeframe, the Board and Team assumed the planning should be ASAP.

As he did with the Iraq Project, Dawson made a big contribution to this one with the help of what he called his, 'Oil Intel People.' He had contacts with people in the oil industry throughout the world including South America. With refineries in Chile, it put some of those Oil Intel People in the right place at the right time.

The Board agreed with the Team's plan for a combination of air/sea transportation for this Project. No problem with the air portion, they would use the corporate jets as they did with other Projects.

The boat transportation was a bit more challenging and how the Team got ashore from the Boat. They could dock at a harbor or marina and the Team could walk off the boat, but ten men walking off a boat carrying gear would probably draw too much attention, even if the men staggered their departures. It would look like a smuggling operation and the police might get involved.

A better idea would be to select a deserted inlet or coastline that would allow the Team to go ashore in rubber boats. What type of boat was the next topic. To accommodate ten men plus two crews, the boat would have to be the size of a fishing boat, but if stopped after the Team went ashore, how does one explain only two American men on a fishing boat off the coast of Chile? The boat question became more involved than it seemed at first, but the Board members tackled it as they had other things in the past and resolved the issue.

After a review of all items, JJ announced, "I think we have covered all issues. Are there any concerns or second thoughts about any of the items we have covered?" When no one responded, JJ then asked, "Are there any new items or concerns?" Again, no responses.

JJ waited a few seconds before saying, "Unless the Team had concerns, I guess it was a go for the operational phase," and everyone agreed.

Before JJ adjourned the meeting, he turned to Foxie and asked, "Do you know how to play chess?"

"I play it, but I'm not very good," Foxie replied. "Why do you ask.

"Chess is a good way to pass the time of day and that may come in handy when we're all sitting in a cell at San Quentin or some other prison."

"Always the optimist," Mac observed with a chuckle, as the meeting adjourned.

CHAPTER TWELVE

J, Mac, and the Team were meeting for the last time before putting their plans into action and JC conducted the briefing. "Since we are using the combination of air and sea on this Project, we will again take off from Mercer Airport using the same drill as in the past. We will run an informal convoy to Mercer field, load up the jet, and Air Jockey will fly the corporate jet to Southern Peru where we will unload and transport to the marina where we will board a yacht. We plan to arrive at the airport in Peru after nine P.M. Less people and daylight to worry about then.

***

JC was right about less people. The Oil Intel People had two vans waiting for the Team and as they made their way to the main gate, they only saw one person. After passing through the gate, the vans proceeded to the marina. It was a good distance from the airport, but by midnight they had arrived, stowed their gear onboard, and Foxie, Mr. Blue, instructed to cast off all lines.

The luxurious yacht eased away from the pier, then headed for the channel. Foxie would head out to sea for several miles before heading south toward the coast of Chile.

"Any coffee on this tub?" Bean inquired

"I think we have some below," a man answered, as he motioned for Bean to follow him.

As Bean followed, he inquired, "Now you're Mr. Puce, right?"

"No, I'm Mr. Black," Gil answered, as he shook his head and smiled.

"Oh, Mr. Black," Bean said with fake realization.

When the two were below with no one else around, Bean said in a low voice, "I get it, CIA, DDO, black ops, Mr. Black. Did you request that code name?"

"No, it was the luck of the draw," Gil assured Bean. "Is that other dickhead going to bust on me about something as well?"

"No, we flipped a coin and Blue Jay lost."

"I'll bet that broke his heart," Gil observed.

"He has been sad since the coin toss," Bean acknowledged.

'*Those two will never change,*' Gil thought, as his mind wandered back to the days when the duo worked for him at the Agency.

While Bean was getting coffee, Blue Jay was accusing Wilson of being Mr. Puce. "No, I'm Mr. Gray," Wilson corrected.

"AKA, The Weed Whacker," Panda added.

"That is correct, Pecker Neck," Wilson replied and everyone chuckled.

By the time the yacht made its turn south, the ice had been broken, melted, evaporated, and everyone acted like it was a reunion of old friends.

***

As the yacht slowed to a crawl, all eyes searched the shoreline for the cove the map said was there.

"Good thing we have this night-vision gear or we would have floated right past the entrance," JC announced, as he pointed to the shore directly in front from where he was standing.

With the entrance discovered, Foxie eased the craft to port and added a little speed to their forward progress. Since he was also wearing night-vision gear, Foxie had no problem finding the entrance, so he entered the cove and stopped the engines.

The Team unsecured and removed a large canvas on deck that covered three rubber crafts. When the boats forward movement slowed to a halt, they quietly put three rubber crafts into the water and attached electric motors to each raft.

Not wanting to leave the rubber rafts onshore, Mac, Foxie, and JC would ferry the men ashore. Team members had been assigned to each raft and were waiting for the word to load.

Mac was at the tiller of the first raft and JC gave the word to load. When Panda, Air Jockey, and Met approached the raft and proceeded to board, Mac commented, "What did I do to deserve these two?"

"Don't worry about it," Panda replied, "just don't hit anything on the way in."

"He'll probably start having flashbacks halfway in, make a U-turn, and come back to ram the yacht," Jockey added.

"Just get in," Mac ordered, "and try not to sink it."

Panda and Jockey were seated when Met started to board toting the drag bag that contained the .50 caliber rifle.

"What hell are you doing, bringing your luggage?" Mac inquired.

"It's the .50," Met said, still laughing at the previous exchanges.

"It's big enough to hold a cannon," Mac observed. "Let the barrel hang off the front. If we run into any hostiles on the way in they'll think they're fucking with a gunboat."

"How did we draw this raft?" Panda asked Jockey.

"You people knock it off," JC ordered from the deck of the yacht.

"Yeah, pipe down," Mac added, "don't you peckers know this is serious business."

Panda and Jockey angled to get into Mac's raft. He figured that's what they probably did and wasn't going to disappoint them.

When all three rafts were loaded, JC gave the word and Mac led the way to shore. The electric motors made very little noise and probably wouldn't have been heard if someone was on the beach. As the rafts got close to the beach, JC was on the com and ordered the three craft to a halt then searched the beach to make sure it was deserted. Satisfied it was okay to proceed, they moved out. When the three craft were in the grasp of the breakers, they all raised their motor propellers out of the water and rode the surf to the beach.

"Can I open my eyes now?" Jockey inquired.

"I think so," Panda replied, "but we better warn them he's on his way back."

"Yeah, don't sink that; it's our ride home," Jockey warned.

"Just get the hell out and push me off this beach," Mac ordered, "and by the way, your reservation on this raft for the return trip has just been canceled."

The three men got out, put their gear on the beach, and then returned to the raft. While they were waiting for a wave to come in so they could float the raft back to sea, Mac said into his com unit, "No unnecessary chances and all you kids be careful." JC and Foxie also wished the Team well before a wave came in that allowed them to be put back to sea. The three electric motors were started and the rafts made their return trip while the Team formed up, moved off the beach, and started inland toward their objective.

With the three rubber craft back on deck, Foxie started the yacht's engines and navigated out of the inlet. With no running lights on, the Team couldn't see the boat as it left, just a muffled noise from the engines.

Following the plan, they would travel further down the coast, pull into a marina, take on fuel for the return trip, then return to the cove and wait. They were just eight rich farts with nothing to do but cruise around.

It was daylight by the time the yacht approached the marina, and Gil suggested making sure no one got recognized. Mac, Foxie, JC, and himself would stay below while they took on fuel. "Who will drive the boat?" Foxie inquired from behind the wheel.

"JJ will take the helm," Mac answered.

Foxie looked at JJ who said, "Been doing it for years."

"See what happens when you assume?" Foxie commented. "When it comes to boats, I just came on like a big assed admiral and took over the helm."

"No problem," JJ assured him, "if this was a bank instead of a boat I would probably have done the same thing."

The two men smiled as Foxie joined the other three men who would go below.

"Now you see what happened when you *assume?*" Mac inquired. "It made an *ass* out of *u* and *him.*

"Just take him below will you," JJ requested.

"Do I have to?" Foxie pleaded.

"Maybe we could just tie a rope around his waist and hang him over the side," JC suggested.

"Gil, you're lucky you didn't decide on a career in the military. See how your life-long military pals turn on you?" Mac continued his attack as the men moved below to wait out the refueling.

With the four men below, JJ arranged for the fuel. While they were taking on fuel, Dunn noticed a few scummy looking men were taking a lot of interest in the yacht and called it to the others' attention. After watching the men for a while, Mac said, "Maybe they are just admiring the craft, but we better be extra vigilant from now on." The others agreed.

***

The Team made good progress during the night hours and after the sun came up, decided to holdup in an area that gave them some decent cover during the daylight hours.

This part of the country wasn't like the desert region further south, but was open enough to make it difficult to conceal the movements of a group this size during daylight hours.

"A combination of wide open and hilly country," Bean observed, as he approached Blue Jay who was checking out the area through his field glasses.

"Yes, it is," Blue Jay replied, as he brought the glasses down to chest level. "I'm just glad their camp isn't in those," he said, as he pointed to the Andes Mountains that loomed in the distance.

"Some of the peaks in that chain top out at over twenty thousand feet," Bean said.

"I think some of the volcanoes pass twenty-four thousand," Blue Jay acknowledged.

The two men looked at the mountains for a while in silence then Bean asked, "You figure tomorrow morning?"

"At the rate we are moving and if our Intel is correct, we should be in position at the deserted mission before dawn," Blue Jay replied.

"Wonder why Al-Qaida decided to put a training camp in this location?" Bean inquired.

"I'd say for a several reasons," Blue Jay offered his opinion. "For one thing, the current government in Chile and they also probably get a lot of support form the tri-border area not far from here. The communists look at the U.S. as its main enemy. Al-Qaida feels the same, so we have a 'your enemy is my enemy' situation like in the Middle East where terrorist camps function in countries that claim they no nothing about it. Another reason could be the terrain in this country. It is a small country, but you have countryside like this. Further south there is a small desert to the East Mountains and you know how they feel about mountains."

"Twenty-four divided by eleven," Bean muttered out loud.

"What?" Blue Jay asked, as he looked at Bean.

"Just thinking," Bean answered. "If Osama Bin Laden was hiding in the Andes, we could take the Team over there, get him, and collect the twenty-four million dollar reward."

"Who are you?" Blue Jay inquired.

"Well, think about," Bean insisted. "Each share would amount to…" then stopped to do some calculations when Pru offered, "I say it's about two million, one hundred and eighty-one thousand dollars and change."

"Thank you," Bean said to Pru then continued. "It's about two million, one hundred and eighty-one thousand dollars and change."

"I heard, I heard, now go the fuck away," Blue Jay replied, as he started to look through the field glasses again. "I don't know what JC was thinking about when he got you people fired up again. I liked it better when you were quiet."

The Team chuckled and since they had their morning ration of humor, tried to get some shuteye.

***

The yacht had refueled and was put back to sea when Mac joined JC on the stern of the boat. He was observing a craft some distance behind them.

"Anything?" Mac inquired.

"Probably nothing," JC replied, "but let's talk with Mr. Blue."

After Foxie observed the vessel, he said, "Well, there is one way to find out. We'll increase speed and head straight out to sea. This puppy has more horses than that one, so even if they are following, we'll outrun them."

Foxie pushed the throttles forward and everyone felt the boat pick up speed.

The old vessel behind them started to fall further behind because they were not following or they could not match the speed.

Everyone was on deck when the boat's phone rang. JJ looked puzzled as he answered, "Hello?" Then said, "It's for you, Gil."

An even more puzzled Dunn took the phone from JJ and said, "Yes?" into the receiver.

"Enjoying your sea voyage?" a voice inquired. Gil immediately realized the voice belonged to Di Flippi and replied, "Very much."

"We almost got to go on an exclusive private cruise some time back, but things didn't work out." Di then paused. "Just trying to remember how that all came about and the name of the company." Di again paused.

Gil's puzzled look changed to very serious as he requested for something to write on.

JJ and Foxie knew it was something important and observed what Dunn was writing. "John's Widow Group Explorer was the name of the cruise company, but before we got to the pier they had already departed."

"That was a shame," Gil replied to the last part of the conversation.

"We were in a rush and we forgot the paper with the route," Di explained. "Boy, was John's wife pissed at us."

The words 'John's wife' ended the transmission, but Dunn gambled that Di would understand a question. "How many people do those exclusive private cruises usually take?"

"About seven," Di answered without hesitation.

While they continued their conversation, Dunn circled certain words on his notes and held it up for the others to read the circled words. Group departed. En route. About seven.

JJ requested the pen from Gil then wrote on the paper, *Al-Qaida group?* and Gil confirmed the question with a headshake.

Dunn continued the conversation with, "Maybe you, Swabbie, and myself could take a trip like that? Why don't you talk to him about it?"

"Good idea, think I will," Di Flippi agreed, as he kept the conversation going for a little while longer.

CHAPTER THIRTEEN

Top Kiner was in the kitchen watching Emeril on TV when the phone rang. "Hello?" Top said, as he answered the phone.

"This is JJ," the voiced informed him. "Remember that special dinner party for my friends we talked about before I left?"

"Yes, I do," Top confirmed.

"Well, I have decided to go ahead with it, but I don't want you and the ladies to go overboard. Just plan for a quiet evening with friends."

"Understand, sir, we'll make sure your friends have an enjoyable time."

"I'll call again to check on your progress," JJ informed him, then hung up.

***

Five hours had passed since Top's conversation with JJ and he was knocking on the front door of a man's house he had never met. When a man finally answered the door, Top said, "I believe you are expecting the Ladies and me?" Top inquired.

"And who are you?" the man asked.

"They call me Top," Kiner answered, "and you?" he asked the man.

"I'm Swabbie," the man answered. "You and the ladies come in."

When everyone was seated, Swabbie again spoke. "I had a visitor a few hours ago that informed me about the situation, so if you don't mind I'll review to make sure I am on the same page."

The other three people agreed and Swabbie started. He first covered the part about the seven Al-Qaida people that were on their way to Virginia. Then he informed the three about on going CIA surveillance at both Blue Jay and Doggie's homes.

"Would they intervene if Al-Qaida made a move on the two men?" Lady1 asked.

"That is a good question, but frankly I don't know," Swabbie answered. "I'll tell you one thing. I'm not going to sit around wondering while my friends' lives hang in the balance. Me not knowing must sound strange to you."

"No, it doesn't," LadyA assured him. "Their actions all depend on orders from higher up, right?"

"Right," Swabbie confirmed. "Were you in intelligence at one time?"

"Both of us were in Intel, different agencies, different places," LadyA acknowledged.

"And you?" Swabbie asked Top.

"I'm just the cook!" Top replied.

"He's more than that," LadyA reassured Swabbie.

"But I don't know what he's going to do without that M-14 rifle," Lady1 chimed in with a smile.

Swabbie just smiled at the remarks and already had a feeling these people could be counted on if the shit hit the fan.

"I think the best way to work this is if you say you are an old friend from years ago when we were in the service and the Ladies are your daughters. From different wives," he quickly added. "The two main reasons for this type of approach are the intelligence considerations, you know the drill. The other being those two guys are rock heads. They are my best friends, but granite from the neck up. They have the hardest heads you will ever see. With maybe the exception of those two they trained. But it would be close."

"No kidding," Top asked. "And the two they trained are hardheads too?"

"Yep," Swabbie answered.

'Food for the Bull Shit Derby,' the three visitors thought, knowing Blue Jay and Bean were the ones in question.

"After we all get introduced, I'll make up a reason to get them back here, then we'll tell them the real story and you can take them out of the area."

"Think you can pull it off?" Swabbie inquired.

"We'll try," the trio replied.

"I guess we should get to it. That Al-Qaida group may already be in the area," Swabbie suggested and the others agreed.

***

Night had fallen and the Team was again on the move. The closer they got to their objective, the slower they proceeded. When they were 900 yards from the deserted mission, they were crawling. Blue Jay brought everyone to a halt and whispered over the com, "Stay here, I'll take a look at the site." He then crawled another fifteen feet and snuck a quick peek over the top of the hill. Not seeing anyone in the immediate area, he went back up for a careful look and to check out the mission that was supposed to be at that coordinates. After a careful survey of the entire area, Blue Jay looked for the old mission. When he found it, he made mental notes, and then returned to the Team.

"The old mission is there. One small building with a very low tower and several other small buildings. Hard to tell how many are in residence. These training sites usually run between twenty to twenty-five people. They are all probably sacked out in the buildings, but two men are on sentry duty in the small tower. From this location, we are facing due east and the sun will not be our friend if we stay here, so we are going to move to our right front so we are facing north in the morning. Any questions?" Blue Jay asked. "None? Let's move out."

***

The yacht had left the other vessel far behind before it turned north and proceeded to the cove. Running a dark boat with the running lights out made it difficult for anyone to spot the yacht. Foxie guided the big boat into the cove, cut the engines, and let the vessel cruise to a stop while Mac and JC checked the shoreline with their night-vision gear. The shore looked deserted so they dropped anchor. "Time to check in with the troops," JC announced, as he went below.

"You out there?" came over the two new longer-range com units that Blue Jay and Pru were carrying.

"We're here," first Blue Jay and then Pru replied.

"We are back," JC said, informing them they were back at the cove.

"Think we'll exercise before breakfast this morning," Blue Jay informed JC.

"Good idea, but don't overdo it," JC advised then clicked off.

***

Doggie, Jar Head, and their wives were already expecting Swabbie and company when they arrived at Jar Head's front door. After he introduced Top and his daughters, everyone was seated in the living room. Swabbie knew he couldn't suggest they all go to his house as soon as they arrived, so time would have to be spent in conversation.

Swabbie seemed to be getting the job done, but Jar Head's wife wanted to include the women so she asked, "You both seem so different, do you both have the same mother?"

"No," LadyA answered. "Dad married twice."

"Is one of them traveling with you?" she then asked.

"No," Lady1 answered. "They're both whores."

"Yeah, Dad sold both of them off to the slave trade years ago," LadyA added, not wanting to be outdone.

Top was sipping a beverage and almost swallowed the glass when he heard the Ladies' remarks.

Thinking it was a joke everyone laughed and Swabbie quickly followed up with, "That's the way their dad was back in our Navy days."

"Ah-boy," was Top's only reply during the entire exchange.

Later, Lady1 asked to use the bathroom, partly because nature called and partly to check the area outside.

When Lady1 entered the bathroom, she closed the door, did not turn on the light, and walked over to the window. As her eyes got more used to the darkness, she thought she saw movement in the trees at the back of the house and focused on that area. She didn't have to wait long before she saw more movement among the trees, but had no way of knowing if they were CIA or Al-Qaida.

When she returned to the living room, she motioned for Swabbie to join her. Swabbie excused himself, came over to her, and had surmised what she was about to tell him. Swabbie and Lady1 pretended to laugh at a funny joke after she told him about the people outside and returned to the others. Lady1 looked at

Top then at LadyA and they both knew immediately what was going on.

Keeping his back to the windows, Swabbie communicated with Jar Head and Doggie. "Just act like nothing happened when I tell you this," he alerted.

Jar Head and Doggie understood and showed no emotion as they waited for Swabbie's next words.

"I wanted to explain this to you later when we were away from this area, but events have changed that. I'll give you more details later, but right now all you need to know is you are in great danger."

"Again," Jar Head replied.

"Surprise, Surprise," Doggie added.

"Yeah, I know," Swabbie remarked, "just like the old days." Then continued with, "We have to make a move out of this front room and into a less open area."

"The kitchen then into the laundry room. No windows and one door," Jar Head suggested, then inquired, "Anyone need a weapon?"

"Never leave home without it," Doggie answered. Swabbie just shook his head no.

"I have some very expensive wine in the other room I would like all to sample," Jar Head announced.

At that moment, Jar Head's wife knew something was up because Jar Head was not that fond of wine.

"Where did you put it, dear?" she inquired.

"It's in the kitchen," Jar Head answered, as he herded everyone in that direction. Once in the kitchen, Jar Head, Doggie, and their wives went into the laundry room to be briefed by Swabbie.

While that was going on, Lady1 told LadyA and Top what she had seen.

When the three men appeared out of the laundry room, Jar Head disappeared for a few seconds, and reappeared with weapons, one stuck in his belt, the other two for the wives.

"How can we tell if they are CIA or Al-Qaida," Top inquired.

"Well, the Agency must be using us for field training," Doggie stated, "because Jar Head and I spot them every day."

"How many?" Swabbie inquired. "It's usually one per shift, per house."

"Is there another staircase to upstairs?" Lady1 inquired.

"Back here," Jar Head said, as he led her to the back staircase. Once upstairs, the two peered out all of the windows looking for the people outside.

"They all seem to be in the area where you first spotted them," Jar Head whispered. "They probably have someone up here checking out the house."

"Didn't they say there was about seven in the group?" Lady1 inquired.

"Yes," Jar Head confirmed.

"Well, let's make it six."

Jar Head agreed and they went back downstairs.

Jar Head told the others what they had discovered, but when he turned to Lady1 she was gone.

"Where did she go?" Jar Head inquired.

"Let me guess," LadyA announced, as she chambered a round in her 9mm silenced Walther, then headed for the backdoor.

"Have an idea," Top suggested. "In the Corps, we had four-man fire teams that worked together or separately. We three have worked together as a Team and you three have done the same. Why not work that way now?"

"Sounds good to me," the other three agreed.

Before he took the same route as LadyA, Top looked at Swabbie and said, "That's the way their dad was back in our Navy days. Ah-boy."

After Jar Head, Doggie, and Swabbie secured the wives behind the washer and dryer, and instructed them to pump holes through the door if a stranger tried to enter, they followed Jar Head to the cellar and up some steps to a door that opened to the side lawn.

While they surveyed the area, Lady1 was stalking the man she and Jar Head figured was doing recon for the group. Lady1 crouched around one of the house corners and waited. When the Al-Qaida man appeared, she quickly stood, put the weapon to his chest, and fired. The barrel was so close to the man, he acted as a flash suppressor and little or no flash was seen when she fired. As the man fell, she first looked to her left and when she looked back to her right, another man had brought his weapon up to fire, but a pop and bigger flash occurred behind him and he was dead before he hit the ground.

"I always did say the letter A was a lot better than the number 1," LadyA informed her partner.

"Get stuffed," Lady1 requested, as the two women continued their search for the other Al-Qaida people.

When the muzzle flashes occurred at the side of the house, the leader of the Al-Qaida group sent the other four men to investigate while he waited in the woods. Three of the men headed for the area where they saw the flashes while the other one went to the other side of the house to circle around and come up from the other direction.

I guess he thought it was a good idea until he met Top and two more muzzle flashes were seen.

The men in the cellar saw the three men come out of the woods and walk toward the house. After a quick conference, they quietly opened the cellar door and took up positions. As the three Al-Qaida men walked past the doorway, Jar Head said, "Hey."

As the three men turned to fire, six shots rang out and their terrorist days were over. The Ladies and Top ran to the location of the gunfire and were relieved their people were okay.

The leader in the woods wanted no part of this, started to flee, and was not noticed until he was a good distance away. "There is the seventh one," the sharp-eyed LadyA said, as she pointed to the man making his way toward a road.

"Too far away," Jar Head said, as Top removed the silencer from his weapon and took aim at the fleeing man. "He's too far away," Jar Head insisted.

"Quiet," Top requested, as he followed the man, then a slight lead and fired.

It seemed like a long time, but was actually a few seconds before the man was knocked over by the incoming round.

"So you do that with rifles and pistols," LadyA confirmed.

"Pretty much," Top replied.

"I always liked his cooking," Lady1 informed everyone.

"The best cooking I ever tasted," LadyA confirmed.

With all of the gunfire and bodies in the area, Swabbie suggested they all get on the road. After some quick packing, Jar Head and his wife were ready to go.

"What about all of this?" Jar Head inquired, as he pointed to the bodies.

"We didn't find any CIA types among the bodies," Swabbie said, "so that suggests someone pulled surveillance off your house, putting you at the mercy of Al-Qaida. I'd say let them figure it out."

"You're right," Jar Head agreed and everyone went to their vehicles.

After a stop at Doggie then Swabbie's house for the same reasons, Top instructed all to follow him. He led them to a small airport parking lot where they all parked their cars and got into two other vans that Top and the Ladies had driven down from New Jersey.

"We're sure these are free from tracking devices," Top informed everyone. "I want to keep you all secure until we figure out what is going on."

"Who are the *we* you keep talking about?" Jar Head inquired.

"And where are those shitbirds Bean and Blue Jay?" Doggie asked.

"Ah-boy," Top sighed, as he closed the side door on the van knowing it was going to be a long ride back to Jersey.

***

During the predawn hours, the Team, minus the long-range shooters, moved in close to the old mission and the two smaller buildings. Not knowing where the main body were housed, they had to get in for a closer look. "Do you have a clear shot?" Blue Jay inquired to Pru and Met about the two men on guard in the small tower.

"In the scope," both men replied.

"Do it," Blue Jay ordered and seconds later two rounds were on the way.

"Both men down," Pru reported on the com and the Team moved onto the buildings.

Benz and Panda were assigned to the building on the right. Tic and Check the one on the left. The remainder of the Team would take the mission building. As the sky started getting lighter, everyone was in place. "Anyone not in place?" Blue Jay asked over the com. When no one replied, Blue Jay said, "Let's do it," and three doors were kicked in followed by men with automatic weapons. Being caught totally off-guard, it was over in seconds. When the firing stopped in the mission building, Blue Jay listened for any additional fire from the other two buildings, then inquired on the com unit, "Everyone clear?"

"Clear," was the reply from the Team.

After the Team checked out the buildings for Intel and other unexplained items, Blue Jay called the Team together. "I counted only thirteen," Blue Jay said a little puzzled. "There should be about five or ten more."

While he was still thinking about it, Met was in his ear. "You on?"

"I'm on," he replied.

"Do you want the bad news or the really bad news?" Met gave him an option.

Blue Jay opted for the first one and Met reported, "You have about twenty men coming in from the east and it looks like another group in training."

"How far?" Blue Jay inquired.

"About one mile," Met confirmed, "moving at a normal pace."

They must not have heard anything due to us being inside the buildings with silenced weapons,' Blue Jay thought. *'But if they try to reach home base by radio, they may come on in a hurry.*

"Don't you want the really bad news?" Met inquired.

"There are another twenty behind the first twenty."

"You're good," Met approved, "you must be gifted."

"No, I ate gypsy shit for breakfast," Blue Jay informed Met.

"I didn't see any shit around," Bean admitted.

"I brought it with me in a Zip lock bag. Keeps it nice and fresh," Blue Jay informed Bean, then said, "Let's move out; we'll talk on the way."

As the Team started to move, Blue Jay was on the com. "We are moving back to the position to the west that overlooked the old mission. We'll meet with you long-rangers at that point. You roger that?"

"Roger," was the reply over the com.

Blue Jay continued relaying his plan to the Team as he moved. "When we meet up with the shooters, we are going to split into two groups and leapfrog out of this area. We'll use the same tactic we used in Cuba with the difference being that time we engaged in combat while trying to escape when the Project was completed. This time combat is the Project and the objective is to take out as many of the enemy as possible."

When the Team reunited with the shooters, Blue Jay divided the Team: Met, Panda, Tic, and Check with Bean.

"Fallback to a good firing position and use the .50 to slow down the enemy's progress. Try to ID the ones in charge and pop them off, that usually slows things down. You know the drill.

"Since we don't have the 308's with us this time, the long-range stuff will be centered around the .50's. Save your MP5 ammo, we are going to need it. Questions? No? Bean, take off."

Bean and the four men in his group started the first move while the remainder took up positions. "Let's take out a few people that look like they are in charge," Blue Jay suggested.

"Have what looks like one of the leaders," Benz informed Blue Jay then directed Pru onto the target.

"Got him," Pru acknowledged.

"Let's start the dance," Blue Jay replied and the .50 spoke, taking the man out at 1,005 yards.

As the man was falling, another one was hit and the entire group dove for cover.

When Blue Jay detected no movement from the first group, he checked out the twenty behind them and discovered they were moving at double time to assist the first group.

"The second group is going to be a problem," Blue Jay said into the com. "When they are in range, reach out and touch someone," he instructed Pru and Benz.

The second group was coming on strong and when they were in range, Pru took down another two.

"Time to leap," Blue Jay ordered and his group started their move. Since Pru and Met were the only two firing on the enemy, one or two of the other Team members would hump the heavy .50 to the next position. That put less strain on the shooters and made for a quick recovery time to get off the first shot at the new location.

As Blue Jay's group changed positions, Met picked up the duties and he took out two more.

The pursuers had picked up the pace. The first group seemed to be newer trainees and the second group was more experienced and had one or two people pushing everyone forward.

The leapfrog tactics were taking its toll on the enemy, but they kept coming. After one of the Teams jumped, the pursuers stopped. "They don't seem to be moving forward," Bean said into the com.

"Noticed that," Blue Jay replied. "Fallback and join us."

Bean and his group were on the move and a short time later had rejoined the others.

"Looks like they are going to change the game," Blue Jay advised.

"Probably going to try and flank us," Bean suggested.

"Probably," Blue Jay agreed, "What's the count?"

Eight and eight were the replies.

'Sixteen from about forty,' Blue Jay thought. *'Better, but still over two to one odds.'*

"Everybody on?" Blue Jay inquired and nine thumbs went into the air signaling they could hear him over the com.

"After taking so many hits, I'm surprised these people haven't given up the chase, but that's good. It looks like they are regrouping and will try something other than a frontal assault, so we are going to change our tactics.

"Pru and Met, continue moving back in the same direction and setup in a position where you can act as both sniper and scout. We know these people are going to try something; you'll give us the direction. The remainder of the Team will set up in defense in two groups. Bris, Tic, and Check with Bean covering the left flank. Benz, Panda, and Jockey with me on the right. Met and Pru will watch the front. If someone tries that approach let us know, then pop them. If they are in force, give a yell.

"Wish we could have thinned out the herd a little more, but they are starting to wise up. It's a little better than two to one in their favor, but we are in defense. It looked like the first group we stung was inexperienced, but the second came on strong. That may be due to experience or one or more of their experienced leaders urging them on. For whatever reason, the long-rangers know what to do about the oppositions leaders.

"Let's huddle up for a second," Blue Jay ordered so he could look each man in the eyes. "I realize this is not the norm for us. We usually hit the objective, then try to evade. I look at it this way. We hit the objective and all of these other fuckers came to the party and became part of the Project. These people may think they are warriors, but they are just thugs killing and maiming innocent defenseless men, women, and children. You are all professionals. I respect each and every one of you and your opinions, so if you have a better idea on why we should not do this, please speak up."

Everyone seemed to agree, and after a brief period of silence, Panda said, "I love this kind of talk. That one was right up there with 'one for the Gipper.' Next time I'm packing a sweater and ball cap for him to enhance the effect."

Without hesitation a serious Blue Jay ordered, "Panda, maybe it would be better if you went with the long-range shooters."

"Are you serious?" a stunned Panda inquired.

"Nooo," Blue Jay replied, "just wanted to see how it felt to say something like that. It happened to me once, but that had to do with a shadow. I'd tell you, but if it got back to JJ he'd have a fucking heart attack."

Blue Jay noticed Tic and Check's look and said, "No, it was another time." Tic and Check gave a look of understanding followed by a look of wonder.

Panda, hearing and seeing all of this, said, "Wait a minute, what do you mean JJ would have a heart attack?"

"Nothing," Blue Jay answered. "I'll end with a saying from that famous German warrior. Disssmisssed," and the Team proceeded to their assignments.

Panda proceeded to find out more info. "You can tell us," he assured Blue Jay.

"Nope," was the reply.

"We'll probably all get killed anyway," he tried again.

"Don't think so," was the next of many refusals to come.

CHAPTER FOURTEEN

Blue Jay took the time during the lull to update the yacht. After JC spoke with Blue Jay, he advised the others about the situation.

"If they are en route, we better get the rubber boats to the beach," JJ suggested.

"The answer to that is yes and no," JC replied. "Yes, we should get the rubber boats to the beach, and no, they are not en route, they are set up in defense."

"Is that wise?" Foxie inquired. "They must be outnumbered two to one."

"I asked that question and let me quote his answer," JC replied. 'I understand they outnumber us, but do they have the will'?"

"What does that mean?" JJ inquired.

"That means they are going to have a hell of a fight, JJ me boy," Mac answered, as he moved to prepare the rubber crafts for the trip to the beach.

Everyone onboard turn to and the rafts were in the water ready to go in no time. JC, Mac, and Foxie disappeared below deck and prepared for the trip to the beach. Since it was open country, and the fact that they might be required to give cover fire if the Team had to break for the beach, JC and Mac reappeared with their M1 rifles. Seconds later, Foxie appeared sporting an AK-47. JC and Mac took note of the weapon and Foxie asked, "What? Everyone else was putting in orders so I asked Gil for this and it's a good one, not a cheap knockoff."

"No problem," Mac assured him.

"It's a good assault weapon," JC added. "If the opposition gets too close to the beach it will really come in handy."

That said the three men proceeded to the boats.

As they were preparing to castoff, Mac looked up at JJ who was standing on the bridge of the yacht. "You look like Captain Bly standing up there."

"Oh, yeah," JJ replied. "Well, Mr. Christian, don't get any funny ideas while you're ashore, you old fuck." Then gave him a thumbs up.

Mac replied with the same then once again led the boats to the beach.

***

Pru and Met were in position and the remainder of the Team setup in defense.

The opposition started to get smart and sent out two men to scout both flanks of their enemy. That movement did not go unnoticed by the long-rangers and the odds were lowered by two.

Getting very frustrated, the leaders decided on an all-out attack on both flanks and moved their men into position.

Pru and Met alerted the Team about all of the movement on both flanks and they prepared for an attack.

They didn't have to wait long before a group came out of the woods on both flanks and attacked. The shooting and yelling as they charged up the hill didn't faze the defenders who waited for the initial amount of gunfire to ease off before they returned fire.

The Al-Qaida group had more firepower, but the Team members were more accurate. The assaults on both flanks fizzled; the attackers took cover and continued to fire.

'Well, this is good and bad,' Blue Jay thought. *'It's good they're not up here, but bad they didn't break and run. We can't afford an extended firefight. They probably have more ammo, plus they could call in groups from other parts of the country.'*

"Cease fire," Blue Jay said. "See if these turds will leave if they are not under fire."

The Team held fire and waited to see if their adversaries departed. After a while, their firing slowly came to a stop, but they showed no signs of leaving.

***

Back at the beach, Foxie, Mac, and JC were starting to get concerned. The firing had stopped, but no communications were coming from the Team.

"Think they are on their way to the beach?" Mac wondered.

"Maybe," JC answered. "I don't want to be bothersome, but will try to communicate if we don't hear soon."

***

After thirty minutes of waiting, Blue Jay motioned for Bean to join him.

As Bean arrived, he said, "Well, Stanley, this is another fine mess you've gotten me into."

"Well, Ollie, we're going to fix that," Blue Jay replied. "Since these people haven't moved, they are probably waiting for reinforcements to arrive. We have to make a break so here is what we'll do…" Blue Jay's words were interrupted by JC's voice in his left ear.

"You there?" JC inquired.

"We're here," he replied.

"What's the scoop?" JC asked.

Blue Jay quickly brought him up to speed, and then advised JC about the firing being stopped, but no one leaving the area.

"They are probably waiting for reinforcements to arrive," JC advised.

"No shit, ya think," Blue Jay had a mild explosion. "I was just talking to Bean about that, but let's make it a conference call." He continued. "Bean, we're going to bring the Team back together and break out on the right flank. You long-rangers will try and slow down the left flank when they start to pursue." When he was done, Blue Jay ended the communication with JC and started to prepare the Team.

***

When the communications ended, Mac inquired, "What he did say?"

"No shit, ya think," a disturbed JC relayed.

Mac figured out what Blue Jay had referred to, looked at Foxie, and both started to chuckle.

"That shitbird pissed me off," JC told the two men. "He always was a pain in the ass. And you two think it's funny!" JC attacked Mac and Foxie.

"No," Mac defended, "we don't think it's funny, do we, Mr. Blue?"

"No," Foxie agreed. "I'm just so happy to be here I don't know what I'm doing."

With that remark, Mac burst into laughter followed by Foxie.

"On the com on the beach, I'm surrounded by shitbirds," JC blustered.

***

The Team was in position as Blue Jay made his final check. "You long-rangers ready?"

"Ready," was the reply.

"Everyone here ready?" he asked, as he looked at each man. Then added, "Let's do it," and each man came up firing and moved down the hill.

The people in the siege did not expect this move, especially with all of those incoming rounds. Some stayed down while others tried to return fire and were cut down.

As the Team's assault moved down the hill, the enemy's left flank got the word to attack up the hill and the first two that got up were cut down. After two more tried and suffered the same fate, the remainder stayed down.

The Team used up a lot of ammo during the charge and magazine changes took place during the attack. Benz kept looking around while he was in the process of removing an empty mag when he saw a man come out of nowhere to the right front of Panda. The man saw Benz was changing his mag, so he went for Panda first. Benz quickly drew a throwing knife, threw it at the attacker, and yelled, "Hey!" The attacker glanced in Benz's direction, saw a knife spinning in the direction of his head, instinctively put his hand up to protect his face, and dodged to one side. The knife spun past his head, but by that time, Panda was aware and took him out.

"Thanks," Panda waved to Benz.

"Was just trying to get his attention," Benz replied with a smile, as a fresh mag clicked into place and they continued down the hill.

Between the surprise attack and the accurate shooting, the Al-Qaida people decided to call it a day and fled.

Blue Jay followed sound Marine Corps tactics and had the Team set up a defensive perimeter in case of a counterattack. "How you people doing with that left flank?" he inquired into the com.

"They are staying put," Met advised.

The people from the right flank were still fleeing when a new group came out of the woods and halted their retreat.

"This isn't good," Blue Jay said into the com, then added, "This must be the group they were waiting for."

"No shit, ya think, you shitbird," JC's voice said into his ear, but it was not on the long-range com.

Blue Jay looked at the other Team members who were already looking around for JC.

"We're back here on the hill behind you, ladies," Mac's voice informed the Team.

The Team all shook their heads and smiled as they discovered where the men were.

"This is Mr. Blue. Thought we'd come out and check on you children," Foxie offered.

"How do you want to work this?" JC then asked.

"If we don't sting them good they'll just regroup and hit us at the beach," Blue Jay offered.

"Agree," JC replied.

The new group had stopped the fleeing men, turned them around, and put them in front of their advance.

"How brave this new group is," Blue Jay observed.

"We'll fix that," JC informed everyone and seconds later, two M1's and the AK-47 started barking and people behind the front row started dropping.

When that happened, the front row went into panic mode and they bolted from the field. The people behind them tried to cut them down, but were instead cut down themselves when Blue Jay gave the word to the Team. With intense deadly fire coming in, the new group also bolted.

"Keep on 'em," Blue Jay ordered and the fire continued.

The left flank got the word on what had happened and the long-rangers allowed them to flee.

The new group finally reached the wood line and kept on running.

Pru and Met searched the woods for those field commanders that always sent their men forward, but never did it themselves. "There you are," Met said when he had one of the commander types in his scope moving amongst the trees.

"Don't hide behind that dead tree," Met advised, as he started his trigger squeeze. The weapon discharged and the big .50 caliber round penetrated the dead tree then knocked the man over backward. "I told you not to hide behind that dead tree," Met reprimanded.

"Well, you spooked mine," Pru scolded, as he followed his commander running and weaving though the woods.

"Very clever," Pru commented, "but you set up a pattern in your running." Seconds later, another round was on its way and the zigzag commander got caught between a zig and a zag.

When it looked liked the opposition was fleeing in disarray, Blue Jay was on the com. "Let's mogate," and the Team started their tactical withdraw.

When they were clear, Blue Jay told the long-rangers to withdraw as well. When Pru and Met rejoined the Team, they all moved onto JC, Mac, and Foxie's position. The trio was watching for any movement and reported that all was quiet when the Team arrived at their position. Not wanting to linger in the area, they all immediately headed out for the beach.

CHAPTER FIFTEEN

With only three long-range radios, and all of them off the boat, Board members were wondering what happened. They heard gunfire in the distance several times then nothing. As most of them watched the shoreline, Gil said, "Our friends are back."

Everyone looked at Gil who then gestured toward the entrance of the cove.

The old vessel that tailed them out of the marina was slowly entering the cove.

"We better not all be on deck when they approach," Gil suggested. "JJ, they already saw you so stay up on the bridge. The rest of you get below and prepare for the worst."

Keeping low, the three men went below to prepare. JJ stayed on the bridge and Gil on deck.

The old fishing boat made a wide swing then approached the yacht on the starboard side. Gil lit up a cigar, as the boat approached and acted as if nothing were out of the ordinary.

The other vessel stopped just short of the yacht and the captain walked out onto the bow of the boat.

"Can we help you?" Dunn inquired, knowing these assholes would probably kill everyone onboard and steal the boat if they had the chance.

"Yes, you can, senor. We want the boat and promise we will not hurt anyone if you give it to us."

"And if we don't?" Gil inquired.

"That would not be a good thing," he said, as two men appeared with rifles on the port and starboard sides of his boat.

"I see," Gil said, as he flicked an ash off of his cigar.

"You seem very calm, senor," the captain observed.

"No, just thinking," Gil answered. "You may kill us as soon as you get on the boat."

"No, no, senor. We just want the boat."

As he kept the pirate in conversation, JJ noticed Gil was holding a .38 caliber revolver in his right hand behind his back. Not wanting Dunn to be blown away by these assholes, JJ spoke up. "Excuse me." And all eyes and weapons immediately focused toward the man on the bridge of the yacht. "Hold on," JJ announced.

"Who are you!" the captain said with a more stern voice.

"I own the yacht," JJ announced.

"Well, maybe I have been talking to the wrong person," the man suggested.

"He owns part of the yacht," Gil countered.

"Well, I think it's best if we just give up the yacht." JJ continued. "These men are armed and the man on the right is getting irritated."

"I don't care," Gil replied. "You only own a part of the yacht."

"But the biggest part," JJ argued.

The captain was getting annoyed at the bickering and yelled, "Stop this," and at that moment, Gil raised his .38, fired twice, and took out the man on the right. As the man on the left started to respond, JJ pumped two rounds into him from the 9mm he was hiding behind his back. The captain dove for cover, yelling for the boat to be backed away.

***

"Did I just hear gunfire?" Blue Jay inquired.

"Afraid so," Foxie confirmed.

"Think it's those people from the marina?" Mac wondered.

"Maybe," Foxie answered.

"Ah, fuck," Blue Jay exclaimed, then ordered, "Let's double time to the beach."

***

The old boat backed away a good distance then turned and ran parallel to the yacht.

The captain took over the wheel and it seemed they were making for the entrance of the cove when automatic weapon fire erupted from the bridge and stern area of the vessel.

"Hit the deck!" Gil yelled.

Knowing he was a sitting duck on the bridge, JJ jumped to the deck.

The gunfire was concentrated on Gil and JJ allowing the other three men to sneak on deck at the stern. The two MP5's concentrated on the man at the stern while Weed Whacker and the Sub Thompson would deal with the fire coming from the bridge area.

The three men opened fire, and what they lacked in marksmanship, they made up for with volume of fire. Within a short time, the incoming fire had stopped.

With his crew eliminated the captain turned his boat to ram the yacht.

When JJ saw the vessel turn toward them, he ran for the bridge. He knew he didn't have time to raise the anchor and get underway before the other boat rammed them, but he could attempt a maneuver to try and avoid a collision.

JJ started the engines and watched the oncoming boat.

The captain was filled with rage and on his way to hit the other vessel amidships when two .50 caliber rounds smashed through the window of his bridge and entered his chest, throwing him back against the bridge wall.

"He's down," Benz reported, "but the boat is still on course."

Gil Dunn, on the deck, looked through field glasses and reported the same thing to JJ. "Do your boat captain shit."

JJ spun the wheel to starboard at the same time pressing the throttles full forward.

The bow of the boat moved a little until the anchor started dragging, but JJ didn't care about that, his objective was to swing the stern to port.

The motors on the yacht were screaming as they tried to push the boat to port. As the old vessel got close, Dunn yelled to the others, "Hold onto your shorts!"

The hardest part for the engines was to get the vessel moving. Once it was in motion, it picked up speed and the stern started swinging around faster. From the beach, it looked like a collision was imminent as the two crafts merged.

It was close, but no cigar. The old boat was so close it left a black smudge along the side of the other vessel as it passed.

After the boat had passed, JJ pulled back on the throttles and just watched as the old boat continued until it beached itself on the shore.

***

It was very quiet on the beach until Mac broke the silence with, "Like I said, Mr. Blue, if you assume it makes an ass out of u and him. Now he's a hero so that leaves u."

"Fuck you, ji-rine," Foxie replied, as he looked at the man with the big smile on his face.

"Let's load up," Blue Jay yelled out and everyone went to their assigned craft.

With everyone back on board, it was time to depart. "You going to drive?" Foxie asked JJ.

"You take her out," JJ answered, as he looked over the side of the yacht. "I have to figure out what we're going to do about all of these bullet holes. It resembles Swiss cheese."

CHAPTER SIXTEEN

J J and the other Board members thought it was best to purchase the boat. They thought about a repair job, but if something were missed, found by someone else later, the action at the cove and surrounding area would point directly at them. Investigations would come to a dead end at the bogus company, but that would just make for more questions and people more curious.

The yacht would be kept at a marina on the west coast and used for vacation trips.

When the yacht returned to its homeport, Mr. Blue and some of the Team went ashore to purchase material to start repairs on the boat.

The next morning, Board members were preparing to go ashore and purchase the boat when Panda spoke up. "May I ask a question?"

"Sure," JJ answered.

"Instead of buying the yacht, why don't you let us repair it?"

"We considered that," JJ started his reply, "but since it looks like Swiss cheese, we were afraid something may be missed, so we decided to purchase it for our personal use."

"That's playing it safe," Panda acknowledged.

As the Board members filed off the boat, Bean inquired to the Team, "I wonder how much a tub like this goes for?"

"Millions," both Tic and Check replied.

"It's good to be rich," Air Jockey observed and the others agreed.

***

Hours had passed before the Board members returned. The yacht's owners were tough, but by the time negotiations were winding down, they were probably willing to pay those businessmen to take the boat just to get them out of the office. They got a fair market price for the boat, but not the killing they were hoping for when the men asked to buy the yacht.

The Board members were pleased with themselves as they filed back onto the boat talking about how the negotiations went. Gil, Mac, and Foxie didn't go with the businessmen to the meeting, but were waiting to greet them on their return.

"Well, it's ours," JJ replied, as he came onboard. "I guess we can get underway."

"Not just yet," Mac replied.

"Why?" JJ asked with a puzzled look.

"Bris is still over the side," Mac answered, as he motioned for everyone to follow him.

As they approached the stern, they could see the Team managing ropes that were over the side. When the Board was at the stern, Mac announced, "The Team figured new owners, new name," as he gestured over the side.

JJ was the first to look over and saw Bris putting the finishing touches on the new name. "The Big Cheese," JJ said out loud, as he read the new name, and then guessed, "because of the holes."

"That, plus you have to be a big cheese to buy a big tub like this," Bean qualified.

JJ and the Board burst into laugher, approved of the name, and suggested a party be held for the occasion.

After trips ashore were completed, that brought back food and cases of champagne, the yacht got underway.

Foxie took the boat out of the marina and set a course due north. They would put it into another marina up the coast before starting serious repairs. Different marina, different country, now a different name, equaled fewer questions while repairs were ongoing.

Everyone was enjoying themselves when JJ entered the bridge with food and drink for Foxie.

"I'll take the wheel," JJ informed him, "have some food."

"Appreciate it," Foxie replied, as JJ took the wheel and Foxie moved to another seat.

"The Big Cheese," JJ chuckled. "I guess we should be thankful they didn't paint it yellow."

"Oh, it was suggested," Foxie told him, "but then voted down."

"By more reasonable thinkers I guess," JJ suggested.

"I guess you could put it that way," Foxie replied. "Didn't know where they could get that much yellow paint."

"They were kidding, right?" JJ questioned.

"One never knows with this bunch," Foxie answered.

"I have to get into a new line of work," JJ told Foxie and laughter could be heard coming off the bridge as the two men continued their conversation.

The plan was to continue up the Pacific Coast to Mexico and the San Felipe Marina in the Baja. Dawson had a vacation house at the El Dorado Ranch Estates not far from there that could be used by the advance group until the others arrived.

With repairs on the yacht completed, Air Jockey, JC, Mac, and Dawson went ashore and started their trip to Paragra to pick up the jets. After that, they would fly to a small airstrip close to the El Dorado Ranch and stay at Dawson's house until the yacht arrived.

A few hours after the four departed, the yacht started the journey to its new home.

***

Dawson, Air Jockey, JC, and Mac were waiting at the marina with transportation when the yacht arrived. There would be no stay over in Mexico. From the marina, it was straight to the airstrip then back to the States.

The four vans arrived at the airfield and pulled up to the two waiting business jets.

JJ noticed everyone seemed a little downhearted as they got out of the vans. This Project had made the Team and Board become very close and both were sad to see it end.

"We'll all see each other again soon," JJ announced and the mood of the group seemed to get better.

After saying goodbye, the Board and Team boarded their separate jets, both taxied for take-off, and first the Board, then the Team was airborne.

***

A half hour into the flight on the Board's jet, Dunn walked over by JJ's seat and said, "We have another situation we may have to consider."

"What is that?" JJ inquired.

"First let me get Dawson. Mac can fly the plane while he attends." Gil went to the cabin and returned a few minutes later. "I'll make this a general overview since I haven't discussed it with people closer to the problem," Gil started. "Jar Head and Doggie were put in danger by, at last count, a triple agent. This agent had access to western Intel and discovered where Jar Head and Doggie were located and passed it onto the terrorists. If Jar Head and Doggie go back to where Intel knows their location, more people will show up and try to get information about us, then kill them."

"Why doesn't western Intel handle the problem?" Wilson asked.

"Well, the French don't know he's a triple," Dunn started. "The CIA knows he's a French agent, an agent for the terrorists, and have recruited him to be an agent for them inside the terrorist network. That's why Jar Head and Doggie were left with no protection. Someone higher up didn't want to jeopardize their source inside the terrorist network."

"I guess their position is reasonable?" JJ wondered.

"I can tell you from personnel experience, triples are bad news. A double you can deal with; triples are usually in it for the excitement or are obsessed with money and cannot be trusted."

"What do you suggest?" JJ asked.

"I'll touch base with my contact as soon as possible and get an update. The Board will have to consider this one very, very carefully. If action is taken, the French will be looking, for obvious reasons and the CIA will be looking because their triple got popped."

"Can everyone be available for a meeting in the morning?" JJ inquired. When he got a yes from everyone, he set the meeting for 9 A.M.

After the plane landed, Dunn would contact his source for an update. In the morning, the Board would meet to consider additional information and to make a decision.

***

The following morning, a tired Gil Dunn flopped into his chair at the Board meeting. With no time to waste, and not trusting communications, he and Di Flippi decided to take trains and meet in Wilmington, Delaware.

Foxie showed up with some much-needed coffee for Gil and the meeting got underway.

"Morning, gentlemen," JJ greeted the Board. "This morning, we will get additional information from Gil, then open up for questions and comments. Gil." JJ nodded to Dunn.

"Contacted my source and things are getting interesting," Dunn informed the others. "The shit hit the fan at CIA about the shootout in Virginia, but the really interesting thing is the triple agent, thinking he had slipped away from all surveillance, had been observed meeting with terrorist network people and not reporting it back to the agency.

"When this was reported back to upper management at the CIA, they decided to let it go on a while longer. My guess is that he has flipped on the Agency. They should take care of him or at the very least somehow let the French know he is a double agent. Since this did not happen, it is decision time for us."

"Thank you, Gil," JJ said and took control of the meeting. "We are now open for comments and questions."

The ensuing conversation covered everything from relocating Jar Head, Doggie, now Swabbie and their wives, to taking out the triple agent or doing both.

When the discussion was winding down, Gil said, "Remember this, we can relocate these people so no one is able to find them, but that triple agent will still be looking for us and have access to western Intel. We are now without a doubt on every Intel radar screen and pieces of information will be floating around the Intel community and that agent will be collecting it."

JJ was in deep thought about the topic when he looked at Foxie and asked, "What are your thoughts?"

"Me? I'm wondering if there is any chocolate cake back by the coffee pot."

"You and chocolate cake," JJ announced.

"Well, I like a break after making a decision," Foxie replied. "Was in Navy Intel for many years. I totally understand what Gil is saying about the triple agent type and this one sounds like trouble. No doubt, higher-ups in management will keep giving him leeway and it will all end up as one big fucking mess. I'd say at the very least we develop a plan to take him out and if needed, move it forward with little delay."

"But how do you really feel about it?" Dawson asked with a smile.

"I get cranky when I don't have my chocolate cake," Foxie told him.

"Have a question," Wilson informed the others. "Gil, you said the CIA should take the agent out or at least tell the French he is a double. Why can't we just make sure the French get information showing he is a double?"

"We could," Dunn replied, "but when I said that, I was giving the CIA's options. I admit it would be a little embarrassing when he told the French he was also an agent for the CIA, but at least he would be off the street."

"Regardless of who told the French, it would not be good for us. In addition to giving up all of his other activities, he would tell about the terrorist's interest in that group that rescued the agents on Corsica. The Al-Qaida group that went to Virginia, etcetera."

"Do you think he would give up all of that information?" Dawson asked.

"Yes, and for two reasons," Gil replied. "One, his track record has shown he will do anything to make it easier on himself. Two, the French have unpleasant ways of getting information out of people, especially traitors, and he knows it."

"Anyone else?" JJ inquired. "No, well I have a big concern before we vote. We have been pushing the Team hard lately and I wonder if it's a good idea to throw another Project at them so soon. I know we gave them the power to turn down any Project for any reason, but to date they have not turned down one."

"Couldn't agree more," Gil said, acknowledging JJ's concerns. "That's why I have developed an alternative plan for this Project, if the Board approved."

"Let's hear the plan then we'll vote," JJ requested.

"As I have mentioned in the past, I have a private source in France that I have worked with for years."

***

Two men walked down the street toward the Monte Carlo Casino in Montico. One of the men was limping and walking with a cane, so their progress was slow.

After looking around for anyone close by, the man without the cane asked, "Boris, see everything you missed during the Cold War when you worked for the KGB."

"I was probably on the French Riviera more than you were, Rene," Boris quipped.

"Probably right," Rene agreed. "When you were here, I was probably in downtown Moscow eating that shit you people call food."

"Frog," was the reply.

"Bolshevik," was the counter.

"I thought you were definitely in retirement after Baghdad?" Rene continued.

"I was," Boris answered.

"Needed the money?" Rene inquired.

"No," Boris replied, "hate people that help the terrorists that kill innocent people. And you?"

"Feel the same," Rene admitted, "but this isn't the smartest thing I've ever done, being so close to my home."

"Maybe you should relocate to where I live," Boris recommended.

"Maybe," Rene agreed.

As they approached the casino, Rene inquired, "Same routine."

"The casino. If he comes out to watch the fireworks competition, even better; we'll play it by ear."

CHAPTER SEVENTEEN

One month had gone by and things were starting to settle down. The sudden death of one of their agents had the French Intelligence Service in a frenzy until they somehow found out he was a double agent and worked for the terrorist network.

***

Rene informed Gil that he and his wife had purchased a house in Switzerland and were in the process of moving.

***

Due to the encounter with Al-Qaida on U.S. soil, the Team did not take their usual time off after a Project, but instead kept a sharp eye around the Barn and the cabin where Jar Head, Doggie, Swabbie. and their wives were staying.

***

All was quiet at the main house until Top and the Ladies heard Mac's voice inquire, "Are you fucking crazy? You of all people. You put all of this together, was so careful about security and everything else, now this. You better go to a head doctor."

Top and the Ladies continued what they were doing, but sort of wandered down the hall toward the den.

Mac was pacing when he looked up and saw them by the doorway. "He wants to have a party," Mac told the trio, "and guess who is coming? The Team, The Board, and the people at the cabin. Our original security is shot in the ass, but you and the people at the cabin don't know the Board, the people at the cabin don't know the Team. The Board doesn't know the House Team or the people at the cabin."

"I feel everyone can be trusted," JJ replied.

"That goes without saying," Mac agreed, "but security should be on a need to know basis and I don't see the need."

"I understand your concerns," JJ admitted. "I'll put it before the Board, Team, and I'll ask the House Team right now."

Top and the Ladies looked at each other then shook their heads in agreement.

"I give up," Mac said as he sat in a chair.

"It will be nice, Mac," LadyA encouraged.

"We'll have your favorites," Lady1 added. "Prime rib and strawberry shortcake."

"That would be nice," Mac caved in, "and maybe some of those little puffy hors d'oeuvreie things? Give me a break, I need a drink!"

"There is something else, Mac," JJ again spoke. "This may be all coming to an end."

"Are you serious?" a stunned Mac asked.

"Nooooo," JJ answered. "Blue Jay told me about the reaction he got from Panda doing something like that, so I thought I'd try it on you."

"You mean the party is also a put-on?" Mac asked.

"No, that part is true," JJ assured him.

"I need a drink!" Mac confirmed.

"Let me try and ease your mind, Mac," JJ asked. "Only code names will be used at the party. We are moving Jar Head, Doggie, Swabbie, and their wives closer to this area for security reasons and we may be moving this home base to another location. Does that ease your mind a little?"

"Oh, yes," Mac admitted, "and can we have some of those little puffy hors d'oeuvreie things?"

Lady1 was in the hallway laughing and LadyA asked her not to encourage him when JJ again tried to convince Mac.

***

The following week, the Board and Team had agreed to the party. The cabin people had accepted an invitation after Blue Jay and Bean did some explaining about Corsica.

There would be twenty-seven people coming to an informal picnic-type affair with a Japanese setting. Benz was setting up an area on the side lawn of the main house that gave both functionality and privacy. In old Japan, the warlords would set up these portable-type units when they were in the field. It amounted to a six or seven foot wall of decorative fabric surrounding a large area. Benz added a top to block the sun or in case of rain.

JJ, Mac, Top, and the Ladies were busy with the seating, wine list, the menu, and those little puffy hors d'oeuvreie things.

JC and the Team worked out secure transportation for everyone and helped set up for the party.

***

The day of the party had arrived and the van transporting the Board was the last to arrive. The huge table was being used for dining outside, leaving enough room to accommodate everyone in the dining room as they were ushered in from the vans.

While some got reacquainted, others were introduced for the first time. Gil introduced Di Flippi to everyone while Blue Jay and Bean did the same with Jar Head, Doggie, Swabbie, and their wives.

After they introduced the trio to JC and Mac, Jar Head said, "Doggie and I are glad we finally have an opportunity to thank you all for saving our beacon on Corsica."

After acknowledging their thanks, JC inquired, "Did you tell them about Floating Simplicity?"

"No, but we'll know it when we see it," Doggie replied, repeating some of the words Bean used when telling them about the Corsica Project.

"We used it all of the time when we were agents in the field," Jar Head assured JC.

"Floating Simplicity," Mac grumbled. "I'm still having bad dreams about him pulling the pins on those gas grenades then putting them back into the box."

"But did you get killed?" JC inquired.

"I'm not sure yet," Mac answered, as the other five men chuckled.

Everyone seemed to hit it off from the start and the party went into high gear after Mrs. Jar Head asked the Board members, "Okay, which one of you is Mr. Puce?"

The Board members looked at Bean and Blue Jay who claimed innocents and Blue Jay even suggested she was a little off by waving his index finger in a circle by his head, until she caught him doing it.

Talking and laughing were the order of the day as the group moved into the dining area.

For the seating, JJ was at the head of the table. The Board was to his left and the Team to his right. As everyone sat down, Air Jockey looked across the table and inquired, "Who's sitting there?" pointing at three empty chairs across from him.

"We are," LadyA replied. "We're sitting with The Big Cheeses."

Everyone laughed as the Board once again looked at Blue Jay and Bean who were claiming innocence almost before being accused.

"It's time for chow," JJ announced, using a term he remembered from his days in the Corps.

A buffet had been set up at the back of the area with everything you could imagine to eat or drink and everyone enjoyed.

Everyone finished dessert and was having coffee when Air Jockey decided it was time to start the Bull Shit Derby.

"May I have everyone's attention? It's that time again, but first I'll explain to the new people. When we first started having these dinners after a Project, it was sort of quiet, but then for some reason this thing called The Bull Shit Derby was born. It consisted of remarks and short stories about things that happened since the last Derby. The ingredients are sort of based on fact, but in a bullshit wrapper.

"We also have an annual contest that I will call the Annual JCCF Award. I'd give you the real name, but there are ladies present."

"Hey, wait a minute," LadyA protested. "You never held back on our account before." She pointed to Lady1 and herself.

"What does that tell you?" Jockey informed her.

"What's that saying about liver?" Panda inquired, already knowing the answer.

"So, we're chopped liver?" LadyA inquired.

"Nothing from you, Lady1?" Jockey inquired.

"I think we forgot to put something out on the buffet. I know! It was the bratwurst!" she exclaimed, as she pushed the button on a stiletto she had slipped out of her pocket, and a six-inch blade jumped straight out of the handle.

"The bad dreams are coming back," Panda announced. "Those poor guys in DC."

"Don't listen to him, Mrs. Doggie," LadyA said. "They tried to assault us, but we just scared them and they ran away."

"I think they passed Guam the other day," Panda informed everyone.

"That was a small example of the Derby and a very small one at that," Jockey pointed out then continued with, "Okay, let's kick things off with the current standings in the Annual JCCF Award and please hold your applause until the end.

"JC is in the lead with four points, Blue Jay is right behind with three, Benz is back to one, and Mac is holding strong at half a point! You may applaud." And the Team gave mock applause.

"Now for the updates," Jockey announced. "Bris figured he would do something different and maybe get multiple points for his deed, so he took on four of the opposition, downed two, then laid on the ground before taking out the other two. **1 point!**"

"Who are these people that cast the votes?" a smiling Bris inquired.

"I asked that last time and got a bullshit answer," Benz informed him.

"It's all fixed," Mac added.

"Secret ballots using carrier pigeons," Jockey defended. "I tried to follow one once with the chopper on its return trip, but the little bastard gave me the slip."

"Moving on," Jockey announced.

"Wanting to get back into the race, Benz talked poor unsuspecting Panda into attacking a force, outnumbering them three to one without using any weapons and were victorious. **1 point!** each.

"We're still not sure about the motive on this next one, but Bean took on five of the enemy and after downing two, did not take cover, and while standing in a hail of gunfire, took out another two. 1½ points. For not taking cover, ¼ quarter point deduction."

Bean reacted like Jockey knew he would and said, "JC was right, you did learn to fly at Pussy Airways."

"For verbal assault on the messenger, an additional ¼ point deduction. Total, **1 point!**." Jockey continued with the report.

"Blue Jay was trailing by one and would not be denied in his quest. For chasing a known terrorist through a small town, causing mayhem, and almost taking out Siwy Accounting before flipping the terrorist and his Corvette through The Home Depot's front window, **1 point!**

"That tied the score, but JC wasn't worried. A few weeks later, during a firefight, he took aim at a harmless shed, fired, and the explosion that followed knocked down a warehouse, half of a residence, and forced the adversaries to withdraw, **1 point!**"

"I can't take credit for that; it was Mac's idea," JC spoke up.

"You hit it," Mac corrected.

"Well, somebody had to. The only thing you were doing was giving our position away with those incendiary rounds," JC said while laughing.

"I'll bet they saw that explosion from the space station," Mac added.

"I'll bet that shed flew past the space station," JC wagered."

"**You ladies!** can figure it all out later. We're moving on," Jockey announced and the Team went into thunderous applause, as Mac and JC laughed so hard they almost turned purple.

When things quieted down a little, Jockey sang, "Mooving ooon.

"The Ladies had an entry this time. Oh, yes, they did. Lady1 charged out into the darkness by herself against seven to one odds, shot one of the them, and almost got herself killed. **1 point!**"

Blue Jay gave JC the high sign then said, "I don't think women should be allowed in the running of the Annual JCCF Award."

"Now why do you say that?" Lady1 fired at Blue Jay.

"Because they're not up to the task," he answered.

"You fuckin' chauvinist pig," Lady1 fired again, then said, "See, Mrs. Jar Head, and you were trying to fix me up with that. I'd rather be fixed up with this jerk," Lady1 announced, as she pointed to Panda across the table.

Panda was sipping coffee when she made the remark, started to laugh, and spit out a little coffee before he managed to swallow the remainder. "What did I do?" Panda asked, as he and everyone else continued to laugh.

It took a while for the laughter to quiet down then Jockey said, "She's a tough act to follow, but here we go again. JC was again ahead by 1 and Blue Jay was pissed. We were in a fierce firefight with Al-Qaida and could have gotten away, but nooo. Blue Jay said *"we're not leaving, so bring it on."* So we waited until they got reinforcements from Pakistan. Since we were in South America at the time, this took a while, but we waited, then we fought our way out. A begrudging **½ point.**

"If my count is correct, JC is still in the lead at **five points** with Blue Jay **½ a point behind.**"

"Dickface," Blue Jay offered his opinion of the messenger.

"With Blue Jay **¾ of a point behind**," Jockey corrected.

"Mac is a serious contender for the prestige LBJ

'Is that guy sucking hind tit award'. To explain," Jockey paused, "when a calf goes between the mother's hind legs to nurse and nature calls, mom doesn't hesitate."

"Know the feeling," Mac assured him. "Get it every time JJ and I talk about Charley Tuna and those weapons we left in Cuba."

"Moving onnn," Jockey quickly said before JJ could respond. "Any questions?"

"How long will the contest go on?" Mrs. Swabbie inquired.

"Since it's the *Annual* JCCF Award, I'd say a year," Jockey replied.

"Boy, he's a smart ass," Mrs. Swabbie said, getting a laugh from the crowd.

With the report of the standings completed, things moved onto the regular Bull Shit Derby.

The Board, Jar head, Doggie, Swabbie, and their wives all got into the swing of things and started to make entries of their own.

***

When things finally slowed down in the A.M., and everyone was exhausted, JJ invited everyone to stay over and arrangements were made so when people wanted to retire they could do so. Jar Head, Doggie, Swabbie, and their wives would stay at the main house and use JJ's, Mac's, and the spare bedrooms. The Team gave up their rooms to the Board and everyone without a bed would make due with the couches chairs or just flop down on the Judo Mats.

In the wee hours of the morning, everyone was still hanging in, but was quieter now, just taking and enjoying each other's company.

Everyone had returned to his or her original seats for a night cap and a cigar. Even LadyA and Lady1 lit up.

"Any thoughts?" JJ inquired, inviting anyone to say what was on his or her mind.

"The Board members have recently discussed your concerns and the fact that it was going to get more intense," Gil started. "And all have agreed on two things. We knew it wasn't going to be easy when we started and the fact it was going to get more intense just proved we are being effective."

"Have stated this before, but will say again," JC started. "I am part of this because governments are still trying to get organized to fight this new kind of war. History has shown during World Wars the U.S. gets off to a slow start, picks up speed, and then tramples over the enemy that started it all.

"When the government finally figures out what they are going to do and gets up to speed, there will no longer be a need for this group."

The table got very quiet as everyone sat back and reflected on what was said.

www.ingramcontent.com/pod-product-compliance
Lightning Source LLC
Chambersburg PA
CBHW052132170626
46812CB00004B/1370